Penny's Unexpected Adventure

Cheryl Wright

 Copyright

Penny's Unexpected Adventure

(SANTA PAWS CHRISTMAS COZY MYSTERY BOOK TWO)

Copyright ©2025 by Cheryl Wright

Small Town Romance Publications

This is a work of fiction. Characters, places, and incidents are a figment of the author's imagination. Any resemblance to actual events, locales, organizations or people living or dead, is totally coincidental.

- This book was written by a human and not Artificial Intelligence (A.I.).

- This book cannot be used to train Artificial Intelligence (A.I.).

Dedication

To our amazing senior dog, Bindy. We love you dearly.
You are a very important member of our family, and always will be.

To Margaret Tanner, my very dear friend and fellow author, for her enduring encouragement and friendship.

To Alan, my husband of over fifty years, who has been a relentless supporter of my writing and dreams for many years.

To You, my wonderful readers, who encourage me to continue writing these stories. It is such a joy knowing so many of you enjoy reading my stories as much as I love writing them for you.

Table of Contents

Chapter One

Hardwick Falls, Montana – Early December, present time

Grace Devlin sat huddled in front of her laptop. Her constant companion, Penny, a small black and white senior dog, was curled up in her luxurious bed at Grace's feet.

Penny was her sister's dog. Kate had unexpectedly passed, leaving the dog homeless. Grace quickly decided to take Penny into her home. There was no question about it – Penny would live with Grace. No way would her sister's dog live out her life in a shelter.

The dog held a special place in her heart – she was the last link Grace had to her sister. The mere thought of it had her fighting back her emotions.

Grace wasn't a dog person. At least she wasn't. Of course she'd had interactions with Penny over the years but hadn't spent a great deal of time with her. Once Penny came to live with Grace, she had weaved her magic and quickly stolen Grace's shattered heart.

Until now Grace only had cats. Sadly, her cat had passed on almost two years earlier, and she didn't have the heart to take on another. Not yet.

She wasn't certain she'd ever be ready. Shadow was a delightful cat. He followed her everywhere, hence the name, and was the most affectionate cat she'd ever had the fortune to share her life with.

"Woof." The almost soundless noise came from Penny. She didn't bark often, but when she did, it was the quietest bark Grace had ever heard.

She glanced up from the computer screen and saw a large form looming at the door. His hand was poised on the door handle, and the stranger appeared confused. He moved closer to the glass door and peered inside.

He then stepped back. Grace could see the uncertainty in his expression. She couldn't blame him. The sign on the door didn't match the outside or the interior. *Kate's Blooms & Petals*. The name was etched in gold for all to see.

Grace wanted nothing more than for this stranger to go away.

"Grrrrrrr...." Penny growled loudly from the moment the stranger's foot landed on the concrete floor.

"Quiet," Grace told her gently, putting her hand to the dog's head and stroking it. Penny glanced up at her, then settled back down.

"We're not open," Grace said, not taking her eyes from the computer. She had no interest in assisting the man, and she knew it was her duty to help him, but...

Besides, Mabel would be here soon.

Confusion clouded his face. "This...this is the florist shop? I mean," he glanced about. "It doesn't look like... Where are all the flowers?"

Grace sighed audibly. Everyone in town knew the situation. Why didn't he? Perhaps he was passing through? It was the only explanation she could think of. "I don't sell flowers," she said firmly, still not looking at him.

It was sort of true, and yet it wasn't. Grace glanced at her watch. Mabel was late. Only by two minutes, but it meant she had to handle this...person by herself.

Mabel was always here by nine. She'd called to say she would be late. But why today of all days?

The door flew open, and Mabel hurried inside. "I'm later than I expected," she said, then hurried out the back. Into the other part of the store. The part where the flowers were stored.

Grace had insisted. She knew absolutely nothing about flowers. Nor did she want to know.

Truth be told, the aroma that filled the store reminded her of Kate. It wasn't that she wanted to forget her sister. She didn't. More than anything, Grace wanted to forget what happened to her.

"Do you, or do you not sell flowers?" the man asked, his hands firmly on his hips.

His voice startled Grace out of her thoughts. "We don't," Grace stated, fully aware she was being dishonest.

Mabel Johnson joined them. "We do," she said firmly. "What can I help you with?"

Chapter Two

Nathan glanced from the younger woman sitting at the computer, to the much older one standing in the doorway. Behind the latter he could see buckets of flowers. There were roses, carnations, orchids, and a number of other flowers he couldn't name. "Er, Nathan Ayers," he said, offering his hand to the woman who still sat at the computer. She made no attempt to move. Didn't even offer her hand in return.

The strangest part was she didn't even glance at him. Her eyes had been trained on the computer screen. If he bumped into her on the street, Nathan was convinced she wouldn't recognize him.

The older woman reached out her hand. "Mabel Johnson," she said. "I am the florist. Grace is only here because she has no choice," she said, bitterness clear in her voice.

He wanted to ask, but Nathan felt as though he'd stepped into a boiling cauldron. Something was amiss, but he had no clue what that might be. "Nice to meet you," he said, wondering if he should add, I think. Except that would be rude.

"Are you passing through?" Mabel asked as she headed into the room where the flowers were stored.

"I live here," he said. "Well, not here exactly. I'm out of town a bit – at Blue Ridge."

Her eyebrows rose in recognition. "You must be…I'm sorry about your father. He was a good man."

"He was." It was still raw, and Nathan found it difficult to talk about. "I've been home for a while, helping out where I could, and learning the ropes."

Mabel nodded. She understood. "Come through. What sort of flowers do you want? They're for your girlfriend?"

"My mother," he said. "She's been feeling low since…" He wanted to say since his father passed, but Nathan was certain he would break down if he did. Thankfully, Mabel understood.

Glancing over his shoulder, he noticed the woman at the computer had gone back to whatever it was she'd been doing. She was not at all sociable, which he found confusing. She was running a florist shop but was not welcoming to her customers.

He found it puzzling.

"Don't worry about Grace," Mabel told him. "She's only here because she has no choice." She leaned forward and breathed the fragrance of the roses. "On the other hand, this is where I thrive. What are you after?"

Nathan sighed with relief. He rarely left the farm, but this was the closest florist for miles around. He'd heard good things about it, but the strange woman at the computer had never been mentioned. Probably with good reason.

She wasn't scary per se, but she was – Nathan wasn't sure what she was. They'd not been introduced, and he decided it was for good reason. "Mother likes any sort of flowers, but she particularly enjoys orchids." He was not a flower person. In fact, he wasn't someone who enjoyed the outdoors. At least he never did before. Since arriving back home, he'd come to enjoy it. Working side by side with his father while learning the business had been difficult.

Not because the business was hard to learn – he had a business degree, after all.

He had to force himself not to visibly shudder. The problem had been knowing his father could collapse and die at any moment.

A warm hand reached out and touched him. "What is your budget?" Mabel asked gently.

His head shot up. Budget? When it came to his mother's happiness, there were no limitations. "There is none," he said firmly. "Whatever it costs is fine with me."

Mabel nodded. The strange woman sitting at the computer coughed. Nathan wasn't sure if she was making a statement, or she had a tickle in her throat.

"This won't take long," Mabel told him, then waved him to a chair not far away. He preferred to stand, and it's exactly what he did. He felt eyes on him.

It could only be the computer hugger. She was watching him, and Nathan suddenly felt awkward.

He chanced a glance at her, and their eyes met. For mere seconds. She quickly turned away. Her fingers were now poised over the keyboard, but they didn't move. Not immediately. Moments later he heard the click-clack of the keyboard. Whatever she was doing before he'd distracted her, she'd gone back to it again.

It didn't last long. She stopped only minutes later. Nathan felt bad. He'd interrupted her flow, or whatever it happened to be. Perhaps she was paying accounts or filling out a spreadsheet. He knew all about that. It was now his job to do all the bookkeeping at the farm. His father had done it all before him, despite Nathan's mother begging him to hire a professional.

According to Jonathan Ayers, the farm was not profitable enough for that. Nathan was yet to lay eyes on the farm's books but would be doing so as a matter of urgency. If the farm wasn't profitable, Nathan wasn't sure he could justify keeping it afloat.

"What do you think?" Mabel's voice drifted across the room. He glanced toward her, to find her holding the most beautiful bouquet of flowers. There was a mixture of various flowers, but above all, the orchids took pride of place.

"It's..." He had to clear his throat. "It's beautiful. Stunning, in fact. Mother will adore it. Thank you," Nathan said. He reached into his back pocket and produced a credit card.

He didn't know why, but Nathan felt at home here in the little florist shop. As his eyes wandered around the small room allocated to the flowers, he wondered why they hadn't utilized the entire store. It made far more sense.

It was on the tip of his tongue to ask, especially given his business acumen. This was what he'd been trained for – to turn struggling businesses into thriving establishments.

Except Nathan knew it wasn't his place. He turned back to Mabel Johnson. "I feel like I've not paid enough," he said. Nathan knew he should just accept the amount he was charged, but it didn't seem right.

Mabel glanced across the room to the stranger at the computer. "It's on her shoulders," she said, nodding toward the stranger at the laptop. She then walked with him to the door. "Thank you for coming. I hope you mother loves the bouquet."

"She will. I know she will," he said. He stepped outside into the cold and the snow, protecting the beautiful bouquet as best he could. His car wasn't far, so they should survive the short walk.

As he drove to the farm, he didn't feel comfortable calling it home just yet, he thought about the woman at the computer. Was she a local? He felt as though he knew her. Perhaps from many years ago?

Instead of being distracted by an unsociable computer geek, Nathan decided he needed to concentrate on the slippery road. The last thing he wanted was to end up in a ditch.

Chapter Three

Grace watched as the man, Nathan something or other, left the building and went out onto the street. She thought he would never leave.

She couldn't concentrate when people were in the store. It was one of the reasons she insisted the flowers were all moved to the back room. The scent of the flowers was the other reason. It brought back all those memories.

In the beginning, Mabel was unhappy about the situation, but she soon became used to it. She didn't necessarily enjoy it, but Grace found the new arrangement more comfortable.

They'd moved all the racks, the paper for the flowers to be wrapped in, and all the equipment needed to collect payment.

Why the store was left to her, she would never know. It wasn't like Grace was a florist. She had never voiced any interest in flowers. Nor did she want to run a store. That's why she kept Mabel on. She was the florist, and a good one at that.

The only problem was Mabel was her only staff. It meant Grace had to be here as a backup. She couldn't let Mabel work here alone. What if something happened to her? Most clients fled when they saw her engrossed with her computer and Mabel wasn't around. Unless it involved strangers. They had no idea and wanted to tell her about their wishes for posies. And bouquets. And even wreaths.

This was not her world. She was not in the least interested in flowers, and she had no intention of changing her mind.

Nope. Not her problem. And Grace told them so.

"I hope you were nice to him," Mabel said, her voice firm.

Grace glanced up at her, but only for a split second. "Of course," she said. It took all her effort not to chuckle.

Mabel glared at her. "Oh, for goodness sakes, Grace," Mabel told her. "I know you were forced into this. And yes, I understand it was not of your choosing, but there will come a day..."

"No, there won't!" Grace snapped. She shook her head. "Sorry, sorry," she said. "It's not that I hate the place, it's just..."

"I know. You didn't ask for it, but you got it anyway." Mabel was one of the few people who understood her. "Perhaps Kate left her business to you for a reason?"

Grace had her own business. She didn't need someone else's business to derail everything she'd worked for. All those years of struggling to keep afloat. And finally, her business was thriving. If she abandoned it now, it would go under. Grace was not prepared to let that happen.

No matter how she felt, or what *she* wanted, Grace was acutely aware she would eventually have to do what was expected of her. She shuddered at the thought.

As if she understood how Grace was feeling, Penny whimpered. She stretched herself to put her paws onto Grace's lap.

Penny was hurting, too. She had lost her constant companion. If she had the power to do so, Grace would wish it all away. Turn the clock backwards and make their lives whole again.

Of course, it was impossible. There was no choice but to accept her new reality. *Their* new reality.

Grace's heart ached.

She stooped and gathered Penny into her arms. Grace held the dog close to her, understanding she must be strong or she would weep. Penny burrowed into Grace's chest, seeking comfort.

She heard familiar shuffling behind her. "Time for a cuppa," Mabel said. She placed a tray containing two mugs of tea and a plate of cookies on a side table.

Shaking her head, Grace decided not to partake of the delicacies Mabel made with her own hands. "I'm fine," she said between sniffles. Penny lifted her head and stared into Grace's face. The dog she saved from who knew what, had a sixth sense. She always knew when Grace was upset, even if she didn't know it herself.

"I'm sure Penny would like a cookie," Mabel said, then broke one of the oat cookies in quarters and offered it to the sweet dog. "She's upset because you're upset," Mabel said gently, then fed Penny another piece of cookie.

Penny scrambled to go to Mabel. It was her fault, Grace knew it was. She was too depressing to be around right now.

A split second decision by someone else, had completely changed her life. She only wished she'd been there. Maybe she could have saved sweet Kate.

She shook herself mentally. Nothing would have saved her sister. If only she hadn't been getting the venue ready for the wedding at that specific time, perhaps things would have been different.

Grace shuddered at the very thought of it. The entire incident was shown on the news. Several people recorded it on their cell phones. Not one person tried to help. It was the thing Grace found the hardest to accept.

Would she ever get over the trauma? Grace sighed. She knew it was a hard pill to swallow, but she had to keep Kate's florist shop running. If only to preserve her sister's memory.

As much as she tried, Grace lost the battle to contain her tears. Mabel hurried to her side.

Waving Mabel aside, Grace wiped at her cheeks. "I'm perfectly fine," she lied. Even Penny glared at her, as if yelling, *Liar!*

"It will get better," Mabel told her gently. "It will take time, there's no doubt. I know the bride's family are devastated at what happened. Not to mention the groom."

No one could have anticipated the groom's former girlfriend would decide to murder the bride on her wedding day. She didn't predict there would be various businesses there preparing for the ceremony. Four innocent people died that day, and Grace knew the town would never recover from such a brutal episode.

Chapter Four

After presenting the flowers to his mother, and watching her face light up, Nathan waited an appropriate amount of time before bringing up business matters.

He now sat in his father's study in front of the computer but couldn't make head nor tail of anything much. The stats hadn't been updated for several months, that much was clear.

"I thought you said the business had an accountant," he said to his mother, although he knew she had little to do with the business. These days she rarely greeted the customers on their arrival. It was the highlight of her day once.

The tree farm itself was seasonal, so December was busy, and the rest of the year was slow.

If not for the café and gift shop, they would have closed down years ago.

"We do. At least we did," his mother said, annoyance in her voice. "Your father let her go. Said we couldn't afford to pay someone to do what he could do himself." She opened the top desk drawer and shuffled papers around. "I have one of her cards here. Somewhere."

Hazel Ayes pulled paper after paper out of the drawer. It was clear to Nathan they needed an accountant, or bookkeeper, and fast. He could see everything was meticulously entered up until about six months ago. It was around that time his father had become ill. Nathan put his hand over his mothers to stop her stressing. "Leave it, Mother. I will sort this mess out."

When he glanced up, her face was white. "I had no idea things had gotten so bad," she said. "If I had known…"

Nathan interrupted her. "You couldn't have done anything. We both know how stubborn dad…was." Talking about his father in the past tense was difficult. His death was still raw and would be for some time. He reached into the drawer and pulled out a handful of papers. A business card fluttered to the floor. Glancing down at the card, he saw the word *Accountant*, in big bold letters. As he picked it up, Nathan knew he would have to rebuild burned bridges. Jonathan Ayes was not the most tactful person. How he'd managed to run the family business for so long, was anyone's guess.

He only had to think about it for a few seconds before Nathan knew the answer. His mother had always been the one who held the family together, and, at time, the business. The gift store and café were both her idea.

His father fought with all he had to stop them before they began. Simply because he didn't want to pay wages. As it turned out, they brought business to the farm all year round.

"I'm parched," Nathan said, looking for a way to remove his mother from a difficult situation. "I'd love a coffee, please. If you have time."

Hazel Ayes smiled briefly. Nathan had no doubt she knew what he was doing.

The moment she was out of the room, he picked up his cell phone and punched in the number on the card. "Hello," he said. "I'm calling from the Blue Ridge Tree Farm." He waited a moment for her response, but there was nothing but cold silence. "I wondered if you could resume your work here. I apologize for anything untoward my father may have said..."

The woman interrupted before he could finish. "He was a perfect gentleman. Said the farm was losing money and could no longer afford my services." Nathan heard her take a deep breath on the other end of the line. "It didn't make sense. In all the time I'd been doing the books, the figures said otherwise."

Nathan found her statement to be most curious. "I'd appreciate if you could come out here and sort things out. There is around six months of details missing."

This time she sighed. "I can come now if that works for you."

Nathan heard the click clack of a keyboard on the other end of the line. This woman sounded as though she was diligent. It was a shame his father had removed her from what she apparently did extremely well. Clearly Jonathan Ayes did it badly. "Thank you," Nathan said. "I appreciate it."

"I will be there in less than an hour."

She disconnected the call before Nathan had a chance to say anything more. Moments later, his mother entered the room with a tray filled with two mugs and a plate of Christmas cake. Nathan would make the most of it while he could.

He was acutely aware the moment the accountant arrived things would change. He would be on edge waiting for her assessment. The biggest question was, how could the farm be losing money? This was the only tree farm in the area. They sold hundreds of trees every December, the café was always packed to capacity, and the gift shop was constantly being restocked.

Something was very wrong, but Nathan had no idea what that might be. His only wish was the accountant was able to find the source of the deficit for him. It would break his mother's heart if they had to sell the tree farm – not only had it survived generations, but it was also his father's pride and joy.

~*~

Despite expecting her to arrive at any moment, Nathan was startled at the knock on the door. He hurried to open it, almost tripping in his haste.

When he opened the door, he was rocked to his core. "You!" he said, not meaning to say the word out loud.

His mother came up behind him only moments later. "Grace," she said gently. "I'm so sorry Jonathan let you go. We really need you."

Grace glanced from one to the other of them. Of course, she already knew his mother. Although she'd met Nathan briefly, she didn't seem to recall him at all.

She pushed her hand forward and tried to simulate a smile. It didn't work. "Nice to meet you," she said automatically.

Nathan didn't believe her. Should he tell her they'd already met? Well, sort of met. It was then he noticed the dog she held with her other arm.

As he reached out to shake her hand, it was clear this woman had no idea who he was. It wasn't surprising. She had barely taken the time to look at him. Did this explain why she wasn't interested in the florist shop? Not really, but perhaps it would come clear as time went on. "Nathan Ayes," he said. "We met briefly at the florist shop this morning." She went ashen, but Nathan had no idea why his words had affected her in this way.

Instead of responding to his words, she changed the subject completely. "I hope you don't mind me bringing Penny. She comes everywhere with me." When he took the time to check, Grace was carrying a large dog bed.

"Of course not, Grace," Hazel said, pushing her way forward.

Nathan watched as she struggled, then reached for the luxurious dog bed. "Let me take that for you," he offered quietly.

They all headed for the study, where Grace placed Penny in the dog bed Nathan had placed close to the desk. Grace sat down behind the desk as though she owned the place. It was clear from that moment she was a take charge sort of person. Earlier, at the florist shop, she was the exact opposite. It was the strangest thing.

"There are no entries for the past six months," Nathan told her. "I don't know why except perhaps Father was too ill." He stopped talking, worried it would upset his mother.

"The profits were diminishing," Grace said quietly. "I told Jonathan I thought someone was stealing from the business. That's when he let me go," she said matter-of-factly.

Nathan and his mother glanced at each other before focusing their attention on Grace. "Do I still have access to the bank statements?" Grace asked Hazel.

Nathan's mother appeared bewildered. Besides, it was his business now and he would do whatever it took. "If you're asking permission, of course," he told her.

Grace nodded, then pulled up the latest statements. Nathan stood behind her and watched over the accountant's shoulder. She then printed out the past year's statements. Taking a red pen, she began to make notes next to one entry from each month's earnings. Without asking, Nathan could see what Grace had found. Only she'd seen it far earlier than he had.

"Would you like to be left alone, Grace?" Hazel asked. "Cup of tea, perhaps?"

"Yes and no. Thank you."

Grace's words were cryptic, but his mother seemed to understand. "Let's go Nathan," she said firmly, and pushed him toward the door.

Once outside the study, Nathan glanced down at his mother curiously. "Grace wants to be left alone and doesn't want tea," she told him.

Nathan shrugged his shoulders. From the moment he set eyes on her, he knew there was something about Grace, but had no idea what it was. Now they'd officially met, he still had no clue.

Chapter Five

Grace was fuming. Six months. Six months!

That's how long it had been since she had worked on the books at the Ayes tree farm. The last time Grace was there, she'd told Jonathan she was concerned about some of the entries. By the time she left, her verbal contract with Jonathan Ayes had been terminated.

Although not an outdoors person, Grace had enjoyed the limited time she spent here at the tree farm. She could work in Jonathan's study, or Hazel would find a quiet spot for her outside. Grace had always enjoyed listening to the sounds of the birds and the wildlife moving around. It was quite mesmerizing.

She worked on her laptop when possible, but sometimes she had no choice but to work in the study. Just as it was today. Grace had no access to the business's bank records from her laptop, as it should be.

As she continued to mark up the printed statements, a pattern was emerging. Right now, there wasn't enough proof of what Grace believed she'd uncovered. However, she was almost certain Jonathan knew exactly what was occurring, but didn't want to believe it. Instead, he told his wife the business was not doing so well.

Penny began to whimper, pulling Grace's attention away from her work. She reached into the large bag she carried with her, and pulled out a portable dog bowl, and a bottle of water. Penny gazed up at her with loving eyes. They had quickly become accustomed to one another after Kate had passed. Still, it had taken Grace awhile to get used to having a dog in her normally quiet home.

The moment she finished filling the bowl with some of the water, Penny took a long drink. Grace went back to her work. With all the markings on the statements, she could definitely see a pattern. Now she needed to get the missing figures into the farm's spreadsheet to bring it all up to date.

Having to work from bank statements was not ideal, but it was all Grace had. At least for now. In the past she had tallied the figures from the duplicate receipts provided to customers. Those appeared to be missing.

Of course, that was part of the reason she'd discovered the deception to begin with. Missing receipts.

Grace recalled the day she'd shared her suspicions. Jonathan was not pleased. He was so upset, he'd decided to run duplicate receipts on all the registers on the farm. When Grace was proven to be correct, he sent her packing.

The response was unexpected, mainly because it came from Jonathan Ayes, a very shrewd business owner.

As the figures filled up the spreadsheet, Grace ran her eyes over the figures of the past two years. The current year's totals showed a serious decline in profit. That could be because of the economy, but she didn't believe it was.

The pattern she'd seen on the bank statements was consistent. In the third week of every month, the bank deposits dipped considerably. There was no explanation for it other than embezzlement.

How she was going to tell this grieving family, Grace did not know.

She leaned down and pulled Penny into her arms. The senior dog did not complain.

~*~

"You're certain?" Nathan Ayes seemed confused.

Grace had been clear in her findings. Perhaps if she said it differently. "One of your staff is pilfering from the business." It hurt to be the one to tell him, but it was her job after all. "I told Jonathan my suspicions, and he didn't believe me." She shrugged her shoulders then. It wasn't difficult. The stats said it all. Someone on their payroll was stealing from them.

"What sort of money are we talking about?" Nathan had gone pale. Not only had he stepped in when his father had announced he was terminal, he'd had to learn his parents' business in record time.

This was the part Grace hated. "Several thousand every month. The strange part is, the theft happens at different times of the month. The deficit is generally only once a month, which made it easier to track."

"And you told my father?" Nathan wanted to know.

"I did, of course I did," Grace said quietly. Did Nathan honestly think it was something she would keep from her client?

Almost as though she knew what his next question was, Nathan asked, "What did he do about it?" And there it was.

"He canceled our agreement." Her voice broke as she spoke the words. It was a terrible time for Grace. She hated giving her clients bad news like this. Jonathan could have fixed the problem very quickly but refused. Instead, he sent her away, effectively making the problem worse. Worse only because he clearly hadn't dealt with it.

"Hmmm." Nathan stared at her, but it was clear his mind was elsewhere.

"Check out the annotations I've made on these statements," she said, handing the printed pages to him. "I went back some time so you can see it's been ongoing."

Nathan's attention was on the statements. "No wonder Father believed the business was not making any profit." He turned to face Grace. "The question is, what do we do about it?"

"I suggest you employ a manager. Someone who understands business, who can keep track of your profits. You need to vet your staff. Particularly anyone who has been employed in the past year." Grace packed her belongings into her bag. She swooped up Penny's water bowl and bed, then headed out of the room. When she returned, Nathan was gaping at her.

"You're going?" he asked as she snatched up Penny.

"Every minute I'm here, it's costing you money," she answered. He did not flinch as she'd expected.

"I am the new manager. I have a diploma in business and have been working in the city in that capacity for many years."

With Penny snuggled against her shoulder, Grace headed out of the study.

"Wait, please," he called after her. He waved for her to sit in one of the comfortable chairs on the opposite side to where she'd been working. "This is not a problem to be pushed aside. We both know that. I don't care what it costs – if we leave this to fester, it will get far worse than it is already."

Grace petted Penny. "Agreed," she said firmly. "Do you have a plan?"

Nathan stared at her. "I was hoping you did."

Chapter Six

Nathan needed to make a decision, and fast. Grace was ready to flee, and he wasn't sure how to stop it from happening. If she left now, the problem would not be solved. It would more than likely continue, and the business would be even further out of pocket. "I know you work for other clients," he told her. "But are you able to devote additional time here? We must resolve this issue. It is the difference between the business surviving or going to ground."

He knew his words were true, but it still cut right to his heart to say them out loud. Nathan only wished he'd left the city sooner. His parents had needed him here. Not only because of his father's health, but he could have helped in many other ways, too.

He would do that now.

Instead of answering, Grace pulled out her laptop and checked...he wasn't sure what she was checking, but guessed it was her schedule. "I can stay the rest of today, if you like. I do have other clients scheduled for the rest of the week, but I can move those slots to later each day. That way I can stay here longer. The benefits of working remotely." She made some entries on her laptop, then closed it up.

"Good." Nathan couldn't put into words how relieved he felt. "Since neither of us has a plan, why don't we take a stroll? You can see how everything works. To be honest, I haven't done much more than get involved in the tree farm part of the business." He glanced down at Penny snuggled in Grace's arms. "You can bring Penny with you."

Grace seemed relieved at his last words. "It sounds like a good idea," she said. "Apart from anything else, it will help me better understand the way the business works." She pulled Penny's coat on the dog, then Grace put on her own coat. Once she was assured they were both rugged up and ready for anything, she headed toward the door.

Nathan was hot on her heels. "We should keep all this absurdity quiet for now," he said firmly.

She stared at him, eyes wide. "Absurdity? I call it embezzlement. But whatever." She shrugged her shoulders, and Nathan knew he was being frivolous about something that was far from trivial.

Grace was right, of course. It was embezzlement, but who was responsible? That was the million-dollar question. Once they found the culprit, Nathan would hand them over to the police. The theft of tens of thousands of dollars could not be dismissed out of hand.

They began their trek to the tree lot. Most people believed the trees they saw in front of them were all there was to the tree farm. With each tree taking around seven years to grow to maturity, they were constantly working for the future of the business.

The first thing the pair came across was the tree farm kiosk. This time of year, they had three to five workers cutting down trees, depending on how busy they were. They also helped customers secure their chosen tree to their cars. Melody stood at the register waiting for the next customer. "Hello, Nathan," she said cordially, as they moved in her direction.

He turned to face her. "Hello, Melody," he responded. "This is my friend Grace." He decided to keep her true identity secret for now. With the introductions over, Melody explained today was a little slow. "It will get busier over the next few days," he told her. "You're doing a great job," he said, then they moved on.

Melody smiled.

Nathan led Grace and Penny deeper into the lot. Grace held Penny close to her, ensuring the dog was kept warm. He pointed out the tree-felling happening ahead, which helped Grace understand the business's operations.

She glanced about. "The café and gift shop – are they one and the same, or different buildings? What about the cash registers?"

Nathan was impressed. The questions she was asking were valid and very relevant to the issue. "They're both in the same building, but each have their own designated area. They also have separate registers."

Their next stop was the gift shop. Nathan again introducing her as his friend. This time to the manager of the store. Damien had two staff working for him today. They mostly restocked the shelves, but occasionally worked the registers when Damien was on a break. He was the only one with access to total and clear the register at the end of each day. He also took the earnings to the main house.

By this time, they'd done a lot of walking, and Grace appeared tired. "Let's take a break," Nathan told her. They entered the café, and he ordered coffee and cake for each of them. They sat discreetly in a corner booth. "As you can see, it's not a complicated set up," he told her. "Somehow, someone has discovered a way to take advantage of their position."

Nathan knew it was true. The most difficult part was going to be finding the culprit. He knew it, and was convinced Grace did, too even though she didn't say so.

~*~

With the tour out of the way, Nathan wasn't sure of the next step. He and Grace had decided to sit down and work out a plan together.

"As you can see from the notations I've made here on the printout, there is no pattern to the deficits. I suspect it's been done purposely, to throw us off the track." What Grace said made perfect sense.

Nathan ran a hand across his chin as he thought about it. "I can see that now. And you are more than likely correct." She might be a little strange, but Grace knew her job. It had quickly become clear it was the case. "I'm not sure how we will catch the culprit. The two managers you met today have been with us for years. Melody is new. Her job is seasonal, but this is her first time with us."

Grace studied him momentarily. "Then we can cross her off our list. The pilfering has been going on for a long time. As you can see here, it's happened consistently for close to a year."

Nathan shook his head. "I don't understand my father's knee jerk reaction. You told him and he canceled your agreement. It doesn't make sense."

Grace raised her eyebrows at him. "It does if he suspected he knew who it was."

Nathan was flabbergasted. Of course. His father already knew who the culprit was but chose not to challenge them. "If that were the case, it would be typical of my father. He would rather lose money than confront the person who was stealing from him."

Grace sighed. "Unless he wrote the details down somewhere, I'm not sure how we can solve this mystery." She glanced down at Penny and patted the sweet dog. "As I mentioned earlier, if those registers have the facility, we can run daily tallies on the machines after all the staff have gone home."

"And compare them to what is brought to the house." This was far more complicated than Nathan thought it would be. Had there only been one point of sale, he was certain they could quickly find the culprit. But there wasn't and they must deal with it.

"You have a lot of staff working here. It's not going to be easy, and we can only try." Grace stood with Penny then. "I don't think there's anything else I can do today. Keep each day's takings separate, as well as from each location. I'll come back tomorrow, and we'll sort through them."

Nathan stood. "It sounds like a plan. Father always just added the takings to the safe without counting anything until he was ready to bank it."

"That may need to change," Grace said firmly.

He walked out with Grace and Penny, a weight lifted from his shoulders. He hoped that together, he and Grace could find the culprit and put a stop to the thefts.

Chapter Seven

Grace felt reinvigorated. She had kept herself hidden from the world since her sister was killed. Murdered.

Her heart broke all over again.

If Kate had died in a car accident, or from illness, her death would make more sense. Or at least be easier to accept. Mindless murder by someone she didn't even know, over something Kate had no knowledge about? It made acceptance so much more difficult.

As she walked from the house to her car, Grace glanced about. With a light dusting of snow on the trees, it was beginning to look like Christmas. Except this year she didn't want to celebrate. Wanted to bypass Christmas altogether.

How could she be happy when her sister lay in a cold grave?

She pulled Penny closer and snuggled into her. Without Penny to get her through, Grace wasn't sure where she would be now. It certainly wouldn't be here with these nice people, trying to sort out their missing earnings.

Grace knew her behavior at Kate's florist shop was unacceptable. According to her sister's lawyer,

Grace had inherited everything, including Kate's home, which was mortgage free. It wouldn't have been fair to Penny to rip her away from the only home she'd known for many years.

The pup was accustomed to spending her days at the florist shop, which was the trigger for Grace working there. However, flowers were not her area of expertise. Besides, they reminded her of what she'd lost – Kate.

Instead, she left it all for Mabel to sort out.

As she settled Penny into the back seat and carefully strapped her in, she thought about today's search for an elusive embezzler. She understood from the get-go this wouldn't be easy. However, she was certain Nathan was not of a similar mind. He might have a business degree, but did he understand figures the way she did? Grace was not convinced.

With the engine purring and the heater warming her up after their jaunt around the property, Grace was beginning to thaw out. When she returned tomorrow, she would ensure she was more appropriately rugged up.

A knock on the driver's side window startled her. She lowered the window.

"You forgot this," Nathan said, holding up her thick winter scarf.

She nodded. "Thank you. I will no doubt need it before I return."

He smiled then walked away. Penny barked as though she too, had been startled, then settled again. Grace glanced at the elderly dog in the rear vision mirror. At first, she found looking after her sister's dog was hard work. Grace had never had dogs, only cats, so wasn't prepared for her new responsibilities. Now they were best friends, and she couldn't understand why she had never followed in Kate's footsteps.

She slowly pulled out of the farm's carpark and headed home. It would be a long, slow ride. At this moment, the coverage was only light. The prediction was for heavy snow.

Grace could only hope they made it home before the roads became too dangerous.

~*~

She drove past Kate's florist shop slowly, to ensure Mabel had gone home. Satisfied, she headed toward her sister's house.

Grace shook herself mentally. It was now her home. Her's and Penny's. Her own apartment was sitting unoccupied.

It still seemed like a bad dream. She pictured Kate coming to work one day, while Grace departs and acts as if nothing unusual has taken place.

Except she knew it would never come true.

After parking her car in the garage, out of the weather, she carried Penny inside. Grace knew it was not good to carry Penny everywhere, but the dog often struggled to walk due to arthritis. At home, she was more comfortable, and wandered about for a short time before snuggling in the extravagantly thick bed Kate had bought not long before she had died.

It was one of those orthopedic beds designed for elderly dogs. While being comfortable, it helped ease the pain of old age.

Grace swallowed back emotion as she stared down at Penny. She couldn't bear to even think about losing Penny. She had become Grace's best friend. Where Grace went, Penny went, too. Leaving her home alone seemed cruel. Especially since she'd been used to going everywhere with Kate.

Grace took off her warm coat, and removed Penny's thick coat, too. The central heating meant they came home to the warmth of a summer's day, not the icy chill of December. Taking a frozen meal from the freezer, Grace placed it in the microwave. While it cooked, she fed Penny.

The black and white dog glanced up at her in anticipation. She loved her food. It was the one thing Grace knew she could rely on with Penny. It was a rare day for her to refuse her meal. The moment she finished eating, Penny climbed into her bed, along with the snuggly toys she'd dragged in with her.

A favorite toy was a stuffed Santa. Mabel had given it to Penny after Kate passed. *After all*, Mabel had said, *Penny was grieving, too*. Grace hadn't thought of it that way. Mabel suggested she take one of Kate's belongings and rub her smell, her essence, onto the toy. It would give the dog comfort, she said.

Not being a dog person, not then anyway, Grace had no idea if it would work. She went from completely ignoring the toy, to taking it everywhere possible.

Mabel was one of the few people Grace spent time with. Dealing with people was not something she enjoyed. Mostly, she worked remotely. Jonathan Ayes had never let her get away with doing so. He demanded she come to his office.

"They are all ganging up on me," Grace told Penny. "I have to admit, I did enjoy today. Despite the difficulties, Nathan made the day bearable."

Penny barked, then curled back up in her bed and closed her eyes.

Chapter Eight

Nathan realized his mistake almost immediately Grace had pulled out of the farm's carpark. He should have phoned her then, but the roads were dangerous enough as it was. The last thing he wanted to do was distract her.

So, he waited.

Almost an hour. "Hello? Grace speaking." Her sweet voice came over the line, and strangely he was taken aback. Nathan had no idea why.

"Grace," he said far too abruptly. "It's Nathan."

"Nathan," she said before he had a chance to continue. "What can I do for you?"

At least he could rest easy knowing she arrived home unscathed. At least it appeared that way. "I had a thought. A couple actually." How she would take this, Nathan had no idea. "First though, I wanted assurance you arrived home in one piece. The moment you left the lot, I worried. This weather is terrible." When she didn't answer, he continued. "The forecast for the rest of the week is for heavier snow. I wondered..." He paused, took a breath, and let it out slowly. "How do you feel about staying over for a few days."

"I…"

"We have a spare room, and it would mean I wouldn't be worrying about you and Penny out in this abominable weather." Silence on the other end of the line bothered him. The last thing he wanted was to offend Grace. "I'm happy to collect you both in the morning and bring you back in a few days when we're done."

He clearly heard her let out a sigh. "That is very kind of you. I don't often drive in the snow. It scares me."

Nathan smiled. He should have known. According to his mother, Grace was somewhat of a recluse. It didn't surprise him at all. The way she huddled over her computer at the florist's shop, not looking at him, and avoiding eye contact at all costs.

He had thought her quite strange, but now believed there was more to it. She had shown a completely different side to her personality out here at the tree farm. It was as though the florist shop itself was a sort of prison.

He shook himself mentally. That was plain stupid. "I have to pick something up before we return," he said, and explained exactly what he needed hoping Grace would know where he could purchase such an item. "Shall I pick you up at nine? At the store?"

"Sounds perfect."

She disconnected before he had a chance to say anything else. Now to tell his mother about the arrangements he'd made. She adored Grace, at least it came across that way, so hopefully she would be delighted. Especially since she had no female company all the way out here.

~*~

When he arrived at Kate's Blooms and Petals, Grace was on a call. He was earlier than planned but had allowed extra time because of the weather. "You can start today? That's wonderful." She held up her hand and pointed to her cell phone. "I'll only be here another fifteen minutes or so. If you can..." She nodded her head, and a smile came to her lips.

Nathan thought hard but couldn't recall her smiling much before today. Hopefully, time away from this place that she clearly hated would have her happy and more relaxed.

After disconnecting the call, she glanced up at him. "Good morning," she said cheerfully. "I've secured another florist." The door suddenly opened at almost the same time.

"Finally!" Mabel said as she rushed through the door. "When is she starting?"

"*He* should be here in ten or fifteen minutes."

The worried look on Mabel's face was concerning. "Do you know this man?" Nathan asked Grace. Not that it was his business, but forcing a male worker on a female who would be alone with him for long periods of time was worrying.

"No, but he's been vetted by the agency I contacted. He'll be here any minute." She turned to Mabel. "I'm sorry, but I'll be gone for most of the week. I have extensive work to do out at the tree farm."

Mabel glared at him. "My mother says hello," he said, and her face seemed to relax a little.

"Please send my best wishes," she told him.

Grace gathered up Penny's bed and the toys she had in it. "She is used to this bed. Besides, it's an orthopedic bed for elderly dogs." Her face was pleading.

Without thinking, Nathan put a hand on her shoulder. "Of course. Whatever you want to take, is fine with me." He took the dog bed from her, along with the toys and carried them out to his car. Returning to the store, he almost bumped into a customer. "After you," he said cordially. The other man nodded his thanks.

Once inside, the man glanced about the empty room. He was unable to hide his dismay at what he found. "Which one of you is Grace?" he asked gruffly.

Grace stepped forward, her arms full of Penny. "That would be me," she told him. Penny growled at the stranger. "Penny," she said, stroking the dog's head. "Enough."

The man looked her over. "Jasper Collins," he said, his hand outreached. "I was led to believe this was a florist shop," he said in disbelief.

"It certainly is," Mabel told him. "Follow me."

"Mabel," Grace said as the pair began to walk away. "You have my permission to change it back." The new man seemed confused. Nathan was, too. "Jasper," she called. "I told the agency this was temporary, but if you fit in, and Mabel is happy with you, it can be permanent if you wish."

Jasper smiled. "That would be wonderful," he said, then continued into the makeshift florist shop.

~*~

Nathan carried the rest of Grace's belongings outside. He placed her overnight bag in the trunk, along with her laptop. She also had a smaller, heavier bag. He assumed it held Penny's food. Grace settled Penny into the backseat on her bed, then strapped her in.

"I know she's spoiled," Grace told him as they pulled away from the curb. "She was a senior when I *adopted* her," she said, her voice close to breaking.

Nathan found it strange. He didn't know much about Grace yet felt he should. Her strange behavior when they first met, and now was puzzling. It was clear Penny meant a lot to her, and yet, it seemed they hadn't been together long. "How long have you had her?" he asked. Nathan regretted his words almost immediately.

Her expression was one of pure agony. She swallowed hard. So much he heard it. "A couple of months," she said. "I'm not sure, it might be more, or even less." She glanced across at him. Nathan was certain there was more she wanted to say.

Nathan reached across and placed his hand over hers. "It's alright," he said gently. "I just wondered."

She turned to face him, but only for seconds. He couldn't help but see the tears swimming in her eyes.

Chapter Nine

Grace knew this was a bad idea. She purposely hadn't told Nathan about her loss. Besides, he was also grieving – for his father.

She straightened her shoulders and turned to face the snow-covered scenery outside. Certain he couldn't see, Grace wiped at her stray tears. "It's beautiful out here," she said quietly. Now more composed than she was before, Grace turned to face him. "Thank you for picking us up. I'm not used to driving on snow-covered roads."

"It is beautiful but can be deadly if you're not used to it." Nathan glanced at her, but only for a moment. He kept his eyes on the road as they came upon the steep curve that took them to the tree farm.

She had driven this route many times before but not in the snow. Jonathan Ayes had never asked her to come to him in this weather. However, she didn't blame Nathan for doing so. It was a unique situation. One she had begun to explore when Jonathan effectively sacked her. "I don't blame him," she said quietly.

He pulled the car in behind the house and turned off the motor. "Who don't you blame?" he asked, keeping his voice low.

"Your father," she said gently. "I believe he knew who stole all that money. Someone close to him, or at least, perhaps, a long-term employee."

Nathan climbed out of the car. He hurried around to her side of the car and opened her door. He helped her out, then stood back as Grace removed Penny, bringing her orthopedic bed with her. "Let's get you both inside, then I'll come back for your belongings."

Hazel stood at the back door watching them. She smiled at the pair. Grace had always got on well with Hazel Ayes. "Welcome, Grace and Penny. I have the spare room ready for you both." She stepped aside to let them pass.

Grace studied Hazel. She seemed stressed, despite the smile on her face. "Thank you, Hazel. I hope it's not too great an inconvenience."

"For you and Penny? Never," she said then led them along a hallway to the guest room. Grace had never been in this part of the house. It was far older than she'd realized. Late 1800's if she guessed correctly. It had been well-preserved and decorated accordingly.

She glanced about the room. The guest bedroom had a canopy bed. It was so pretty, and Grace couldn't wait to sleep in it. If she could sleep, that is. Her broken heart had made sleep evasive. Perhaps because she slept in the bed her sister had slept in for several years. Maybe it was a bad idea moving into Kate's place.

She did it for Penny.

As she continued to look around, Grace couldn't help but notice the entire room had been fitted out in a Victorian theme. All the furniture was from the era, including the sofa which was covered in a pretty floral pattern.

In the corner was a bowl and jug, sitting on top of a cupboard. The wardrobe in the corner was a perfect representation of the late 1800's, even if she suspected everything to be reproductions. It had a homely feeling about it, and Grace immediately felt comfortable here.

It wasn't long before Nathan entered the room with her belongings. He placed them on the floor next to the wardrobe. "What do you think?" he asked Grace. "It is Mother's pride and joy."

Grace couldn't help but feel relaxed and happy in this room. "It is quite beautiful," she said, before walking over to the window to check out the view. Even the view from the back of the house was stunning. Grace had no idea Christmas trees grew there too. She turned to face Nathan and Hazel. "This is all part of your farm?" she asked.

"We own several acres of land," Nathan told her. "The homestead has been here far longer than the tree farm. My grandfather bought the property and grew the first lot of trees. While those trees were growing, he planted the next acre of trees." He glanced across at his mother. "Father took it over when he married Mother. It is very special to our family, but a lot of work," he added.

"I can only imagine. I had no idea your land was this big." She had never been given a tour of the property. Then again, money had not gone missing before. "Did you want to get started now?" she asked Nathan.

"Let's have a coffee first. It was a long drive given the snow-covered roads." He glanced at Hazel who disappeared out of the room. "After that, it could be an even longer day."

It was already turning out to be a long day. Not only had Grace agreed to leave home for a few days, she had given Mabel permission to restore Kate's florist shop back to the way it had been before.

The way it was before Kate died.

~*~

Hazel arrived with morning tea in the midst of their discussion. Nathan immediately stopped talking. Grace said nothing, but it was clear he didn't want to involve his mother in the technicalities of the embezzlement.

She had never been involved in the business side of the tree farm, as far as Grace could tell. But she could be wrong. Grace had been working with Jonathan for only a few years. What happened before then, she had no idea.

"Thank you, Hazel," she said. "It's been one of those days. And that was before Nathan arrived for Penny and me."

Hazel stared at her. "As if you don't have enough on your plate already."

Grace shook her head. "It isn't like that. I finally gave in and hired a new florist. He started this morning and is on a trial for now."

"No one will ever replace..." Hazel let her words trail off, then hurried out of the room.

It wasn't about replacing Kate. This was more about letting go. Handing the store over to Mabel and whomever else she hired to run the store. Whether that was Jasper Collins or someone else, Grace didn't as yet know.

What had become abundantly clear, was she had to distance herself from her dear sister's business. Already a recluse of sorts before the tragedy, she'd become worse since setting herself up in the store.

Working from her own home office had been far better for her mental health. Living in Kate's home had not helped either.

Grace knew she had a lot of thinking to do. For now, though, she had to help Nathan solve the dilemma of who was stealing from him.

Chapter Ten

Nathan's gaze went from his mother to Grace. He was missing something, but what it was, he had no idea.

Almost the moment they finished their coffee, he led Grace into the study. "There is clearly no pattern," he said. "Although I believe we already established that thought."

Grace stared down at the printed statements. "The only pattern I see is whomever is stealing from you is making it look random." He was staring at her but couldn't help it. Something seemed off. He'd already established Grace was different, although when it came to her work, she was spot on.

He glanced across at the shopping bag sitting on his father's desk. It was now Nathan's desk, but he preferred to call it Grace's desk. At least for now. She was sitting in front of Father's computer, so it was a valid call.

"We'll stop for a break, if that works for you," he said. It felt as though they were going over the same thing every time they studied the statements. Grace had told him so, but Nathan was certain he was missing something.

Grace nodded, then stood. The pair moved to the low table at the side of the room. His father insisted he have a place where he could drink coffee and relax. Sometimes Hazel joined him, other times he sat there alone.

"I can feel your Father looking over my shoulder when I sit at his desk," she said quietly, moments before she shivered.

Nathan stared at her. She really was quite strange.

"He certainly was a strong personality. I just wish he'd made a note about who he believed was pilfering." More than ever, Nathan believed it was someone close to Jonathan Ayes. Otherwise, he would surely have called in the police. None of it made sense. And that had him flummoxed.

Nathan picked up a plate of Christmas cake and offered a slice to Grace. "Mother made this yesterday," he said. "It's delicious."

She reached out and took a slice, adding it to the small plate provided. Grace came across as a delicate person. He didn't know why, but it was there slightly beneath the surface. When it came to her work, she was fierce. Except he'd seen the other side of her. The side that huddled over her laptop, not making eye contact with anyone. Not even her employee.

And what was up with having that entire room empty of flowers? Mother obviously knew, but Grace wasn't letting on. It was entirely her prerogative.

"I guess you're changing up the system," she said, glancing at the shopping bag. "How will it work? Or would you rather not say?"

He leaned in and whispered close to her ear. "I'll collect the cash from each arm of the business at the end of each day. Those bags, as you know, have locks. They will be placed in the safe immediately after we've counted the money to tally with the cash register receipts."

Grace frowned. Then stared at him. He had no idea who was stealing the money, and was grasping at straws. "That's a lot of extra work for you," she said quietly.

It truly was, but Nathan hoped it would be worth it in the end.

"I checked some things out last night after I got home," she said, keeping her voice low. "I believe those cash registers can be linked to your computer."

Nathan's heart pounded. "Does that mean we can check the details remotely?" He kept his voice as low as possible.

"It depends on the model, from what I can tell. Perhaps we can find the receipts, or simply go to each store and check for ourselves?"

She wiped a hand across her forehead, pushing back a loose tendril of hair. He'd never really taken a lot of notice of Grace's looks before, but now, with working so close with her, he could see her vulnerability. "I believe the registers were replaced in the past year. Fingers crossed they do what you believe."

Grace took a long draw of her coffee, then wiped her lips with a napkin. She finished off her cake, then discovered the cookie Hazel had placed on the plate for Penny. Her face lit up. It seemed to Nathan, Penny was her whole world. Surely, she had family.

Except she'd told him Penny was a senior whose owner had recently passed. Could that owner have been a friend? Or even family? It made him wonder if loss contributed to her curious behavior. Grace took Penny everywhere. She rarely put the dog to the floor to walk, just carried her carefully as if worried she would break.

As if Penny was the last link to whomever she'd belonged to before. His heart sank. She was grieving. Why he hadn't seen it before, Nathan didn't know.

He should have seen the signs. Especially since he'd been there so recently himself. He'd watched his mother go through the same thing, only it wasn't as severe. Perhaps because she'd had prior warning. They all knew what was coming. What to expect.

Nathan wanted to pull Grace into his arms and hold her until her pain all disappeared. Except he couldn't do that. It would be inappropriate. Besides, it wouldn't work beyond a few minutes at most.

He only wished his mother had told him. Before he'd asked Grace to drive all the way out here to assist.

One thing Nathan was certain about, was the business was not on the brink of collapse. Most of the numbers supported his conclusion. It was only those pesky drops around once a month. It appeared the money was being stolen before it was put in the safe.

There was no other explanation. Or was there?

What happened to you? he wanted to ask Grace. Instinctively, he knew whatever she'd endured, Penny had, too. They were going through it together. No wonder Grace wouldn't let Penny out of her sight.

He watched as she trotted over to Penny's bed and brought the dog back. She proceeded to break the cookie into quarters for the elderly dog.

Penny gobbled it up, thoroughly enjoying the treat. Grace's face lit up seeing the dog's joy. "She loves your mother's cookies," Grace said. "I should make some for her, but I'm not that good of a cook." She seemed disappointed. "My sister, on the other hand..." Grace abruptly stopped talking.

Her sister? It was the first he'd heard of the existence of a sister. Although it wasn't like he should have. They barely knew each other. "We can't all be good at everything," Nathan said, trying to make light of what seemed a difficult situation.

He didn't want to ask. She was clearly in pain. Nathan could ask his mother, but that wouldn't be fair. It wasn't any of his business. If Grace wanted to tell him, she surely would.

Chapter Eleven

Grace swallowed back her emotions. For a moment there, she'd almost forgotten Kate was gone. Her heart thudded, and she felt lightheaded. If she didn't have Penny on her lap, she may have succumbed. Only she had to protect Penny at all costs.

She also didn't want to make a fool of herself in front of Nathan. Who was, after all a stranger. He might be Jonathan's son, but that didn't automatically make him trustworthy. If Hazel hadn't been in the house, she would not have agreed to stay.

At least Nathan had the foresight to ask her to stay over. The weather was already bleak, and glancing out the window, she could see the snow was heavier than when they arrived. Christmas was creeping up on them. Faster than she would like.

How would she cope without Kate? Her future looked bleak. The thought rocked Grace to her core.

Suddenly a whirlwind ran through the room. It moved so quickly, and she had no idea what it was. Until she heard a tiny bark.

"Arnie!" Nathan growled. "Sorry, he is a ball of energy." He leaned down and picked up the energetic pup.

"I've never seen him before." It seemed strange to Grace that there was a dog in the house, and they hadn't even crossed paths.

"Father got him for my mother. He didn't want her to be lonely after he was gone. As you can see, he is rather rambunctious."

Grace leaned across the table and petted the ball of fluff. "He's adorable," she said, then took Penny back to her bed not far away.

Without warning, Arnie jumped from Nathan's lap and headed toward Penny. "Arnie, no!" Nathan shouted. But he took no notice.

Arnie climbed into Penny's bed. He rubbed his little head against Penny's, and the pair stayed like that for more than a minute. It was like Arnie knew Penny was grieving. Grace knew dogs had a sixth sense, but this was almost beyond belief.

She stayed rooted to her spot, focusing entirely on the dogs. There was silence all around her, and Grace was speechless. Arnie obviously knew Penny needed comforting and wanted to provide it.

Her heart raced. Everywhere she turned, there were reminders of what she was missing. Who she was missing with all her heart.

Without warning, Nathan was sitting next to her. His fingers gently wiped her cheeks. He didn't say a word but pulled Grace against him. Wrapped her in his arms. "You don't have to say anything," he said. "We can sit here for as long as you want."

Grace nodded and leaned into him. This was the first time she'd felt real comfort since she'd lost her precious sister.

Tears continued to fall, and Nathan continued to wipe them away and hold her close. Grace owed him an explanation. She forced herself away from the comfort of his arms and whispered the words she never thought she would have to say. "My sister was murdered," she whispered. "About two months ago. Penny was her dog."

"I'm truly sorry," Nathan said, pulling her close again. "You inherited the florist shop?"

This time Grace nodded. She was completely drained. How she could continue working after this, she didn't know.

"Why don't we get some fresh air?" Nathan suggested. It sounded like a good idea. "It's stopped snowing for now. Would Penny like to walk? I know Arnie would."

"Some days Penny can walk a short distance, but others, not much at all."

"Arthritis?" Nathan asked.

She nodded again. It was inevitable she would lose Penny in old age. Being a senior already, Grace knew their time together was limited.

They prepared both dogs to go outside. Penny was wrapped in her winter coat and had her harness on. Arnie was a little harder to prepare. He was a typical pup – over excited, and a bundle of energy. Grace helped Nathan get Arnie's winter coat on, along with his little snow booties, not surprised it took two of them to handle the pup.

They stuck their heads in the kitchen to tell Hazel they were going out with the dogs. Hazel's expression turned speculative. Grace wasn't sure what that was all about.

The moment they stepped outside in their thick coats, gloves, and scarves, the icy air hit her in the face. It was exactly what Grace needed. They'd pored over the books all morning, and needed to clear their heads.

Now they were outside and alone, she expressed curiosity about the lockable cash bags.

"An additional security check," he told her. "I've decided to collect the cash from each vendor, instead of them coming to me."

Grace was confused. She understood they'd taken the cash to the house all these years.

Nathan clearly saw her confusion. "What if the money is going missing between the store and the house? It's a small deviation from our protocols, but I have a theory, and I'd like to see it play out."

"Can I make a suggestion?" she asked gently. "Why not do what you said, except use the regular cash bags. That way you're not changing much, and not alerting the culprit you're on to them."

Nathan rubbed his chin. "I see your point. Yes, let's do that. It actually might work better."

They hadn't gone far when Penny suddenly sat down. "That's her done," Grace told him. "She can't walk far these days." Leaning down, Grace swooped the senior dog up into her arms.

"About those cash registers," Nathan said carefully. "Could you look into whether ours can be viewed on the business's central computer? It's another check on what's happening."

Grace was glad to see Nathan was prepared to go all out with this investigation. "Of course. I just need the brand and model of the registers. I suggest we do it quietly and without any fanfare."

Nathan studied her momentarily. "Agreed," he finally said.

Why alert the thief to the fact they were checking into the missing money? As far as the person embezzling the money was concerned, their transgressions had not been discovered. Except they had, and Grace felt they were getting closer to a resolution by the hour.

Chapter Twelve

Nathan glanced at Grace. It all began to make sense – her strange behavior at the florist shop, her change of personality, and her concerns over Penny.

Frankly, he didn't blame her. Now, he felt bad asking her to stay on the farm for the rest of the week, but it was in her best interest. Driving for at least an hour each day would not be good for her either.

Besides, it may help with her grieving process. Clearly the florist shop was making things worse for her. He glanced across and smiled at the look of content on Penny's little face. Even Grace seemed a little more relaxed.

"These trees are magical," she said.

Nathan couldn't argue. The entire lot seemed magical when it snowed, whether it was a light spattering or a heavy downfall. "It is truly a sight to behold," he told her. "In hindsight, I wished I'd stayed on, and not left to work in the city."

Grace put a hand to his well-padded arm. "I know what you mean. I left Hardwick Falls to do my accounting training. It took a few years, but it meant I lost time with my sister." She swallowed down hard, and Nathan knew she was fighting back her emotions.

"The trouble is, we can't foresee the future. Father wasn't very old. It was simply bad luck he became ill. He succumbed quickly to his illness."

"My sister didn't stand a chance," Grace said, fighting back tears. "She was gunned down by a complete stranger."

"In the florist shop?" Nathan asked, his voice incredulous.

"She was at a wedding venue, setting up the floral arrangements." She sighed, and Nathan instinctively knew she believed it was pure bad luck. "Wrong place, wrong time," she finally said.

He had no response for that. Grace was completely right. Nathan glanced at the pup on the other end of the leash. Arnie was sniffing everything in his path. It was not surprising, since this was all new territory for him. Hazel did not walk the dog often, and Nathan had been tied up trying to sort out the business.

"He's adorable," Grace said, following his line of vision.

Nathan couldn't help but smile. The pup really was adorable. "Penny is cute, too. I can't believe she's a senior."

Grace stared down at the fluffy bundle in her arms. "I can't either. Our time together is limited," she said quietly. "We're living at my sister's house. I thought it would be easier on Penny." She glanced down at Penny briefly. "It's one of the most difficult things I've ever done."

Nathan could understand that. He hesitated before responding. "Could you live elsewhere?" he asked gently.

"I still have my own place. I'd rather be there. At Kate's house there are too many ghosts. Too many memories."

"I get it," Nathan said. "I really do. Except I've barely visited here over the past years. Only a few times a year. Mostly for the holidays."

It wasn't long before they arrived at the tree farm arm of the business. Melody was busy taking payments, so they waited off to the side.

"I was sorry to hear about your dad," one customer said, shaking Nathan's hand. It wasn't long before a number of customers did the same.

"Thanks everyone. I will pass on your condolences to my mother." It was inevitable, Nathan knew. But knowing Grace's situation, he felt bad for her. Finally, the clump of customers disappeared into the farm, looking for the perfect tree.

"How are you coping, Melody," Nathan asked. Her expression was one of a deer in headlights. "Do you need additional help?"

While Nathan chatted with Melody, Grace stepped closer to the cash register and discreetly looked it over. After reassurance from Melody there was no need for additional staff at this point, they headed toward the gift shop.

"Melody," Nathan said, suddenly remembering one of the reasons for this visit. "I will collect the takings at the end of the day. No need for you to come to the homestead."

She looked relieved. "Thank you," Melody told him. "I do feel vulnerable carrying that amount of money alone."

It went far more smoothly than he expected. Now to the gift shop.

~*~

"We're back," Nathan said as he popped his head around the doorway to the kitchen. "Something smells good."

Instead of retreating to the study, as he'd originally planned, he stepped further into the kitchen. Hazel glanced across the room at him and smiled. "Did you have a nice walk? Was Arnie a good boy?" she asked.

"Arnie is still learning how to walk politely, but he was pretty good for his age." Nathan released Arnie from his harness, and the pup did zoomies across the kitchen floor.

"Arnie!" Nathan said firmly. The pup immediately stopped, then turned to Nathan with a sad expression on his face. "We've talked about this before, Arnie. Zoomies in the house are not acceptable." Now the pup appeared downright guilty. As he was.

When Nathan glanced across at Grace, she was trying to hide her grin behind her hand. It didn't work. As she held Penny in her arms, Grace began to giggle. It caused Nathan to grin, and then he broke out in laughter. "It's not funny," he tried to say in a serious voice. He completely failed.

"Then why are you laughing?" Grace demanded, still giggling.

When he glanced at his mother, she, too, was laughing. "It's so nice to laugh again," Hazel said, wiping tears from her eyes. "It's been awhile."

"It has," Nathan told her.

Grace stepped back, moving out of the kitchen. Nathan could see it on her face – this, to her, was a family moment, and she didn't belong. Except she did belong. Grace felt more like family than some members of his family.

It was crazy. She was their accountant, not blood. And once they'd solved the mystery of the missing money, Grace would go back to her life in Hardwick Falls.

The very thought of it had him feeling depressed.

Chapter Thirteen

Grace quickly stepped backwards out of the kitchen, leaving Nathan and his mother alone. This was a moment they should share together, not with someone they barely knew.

She turned around, heading back to the study, certain they were missing something. Now she had all the details of the registers, she could check if these registers could be linked to a central computer. Whether that helped their cause, Grace wasn't sure. At least it would feel like they were doing something proactive.

"Grace." Nathan's voice wasn't far behind her, and she cringed. Not because he was calling to her. She didn't want him feeling bad about her retreating from a private moment between Nathan and Hazel.

She turned to face him and noticed his frown. "Nathan," she said, mimicking him. "I was going to research the registers." She began to walk away again, more determined this time.

"I'll come with you," he said, and fell into step beside her. Already, Grace could foresee a problem. The register for the tree farm itself was much older. The rest of the business came much later, meaning those registers were far more modern.

Upon reaching the study, Grace placed Penny in her bed. Once settled in front of the computer, Grace did a google search. She added the details of the two newer registers and was relieved they could be linked. Unfortunately, the oldest one could not.

"They are not a cheap item," she told Nathan after disclosing the results she'd found. "You need to assess if it's worth the money to have them all the same and get stats in real time." Nathan studied her as he thought on her words. "On the other hand, you've already lost tens of thousands of dollars."

Nathan cringed. But not for long. "You're right," he said quietly. "Let's buy a new register for the tree farm, to bring them all in line. That's the excuse we'll use, anyway," he said.

"Should I order one now, or…"

He cut her off before Grace could continue. "Order it now. No point in delaying the inevitable. We won't mention any of this to anyone. Okay?"

"Not even to your mother?" Grace could understand his reasoning. Hazel was already stressed about the business, so why add to her anxiety?

"Not even to Mother. She's not involved in the business in any way."

Grace found the best price and ordered express delivery. She also ordered the software required for the real time stats they needed. "This will be a game changer," she told Nathan, then leaned back in her chair and sighed. She hoped this would be the beginning of the end for the person stealing from this family business.

"I don't know if this will work," Grace told him, "but we can only try."

They both turned as the whirlwind known as Arnie flew into the study. He went straight to Penny's bed and curled up next to her. Penny did not flinch. Nor did she bat an eyelid.

"Perhaps Arnie is what she needs," Nathan said as he studied the pair. "And maybe, just maybe, Arnie needs Penny, too. He lost someone as well."

Grace's heart thudded. Of course. Jonathan bought Arnie for his wife some time before he passed. "I would like to think you're right," she said. "Thank you for being there for me earlier. I guess I needed someone to lean on."

"We all need a shoulder to cry on at some time. Or an ear to listen."

Grace knew Nathan was right. However, showing her emotions to a person she barely knew did not sit well with Grace.

The ding on the computer startled her. "It's here. The new software package has arrived," she said.

"Weather permitting, the new register should be here tomorrow." Grace sighed with relief. It was all coming together. She was almost certain they wouldn't pinpoint the culprit before she went back home at the end of the week. But they would have a decent start to making that happen.

She set about installing the software, with Nathan watching over her shoulder. When she was gone, it would be his responsibility to manage and oversee the system. His staff would be none the wiser.

Grace logged on and set up the software. Next, they needed the serial numbers of the existing registers to get their stats rolling in. "We can have it go back as far as you want," Grace said, turning to Nathan.

"Take it back to where the money began to disappear. No, wait." He thought deeply for a minute. "Let's take it back to the start of the year. That's when we know it was definitely a problem. We can change the date range later if we want, right?"

"Right," Grace said. "I've retrieved the serial numbers for the existing registers from the company's website. We can add the new register when it arrives, and we have the serial number."

Nathan shook his head. "I don't know what we would do without you, Grace. You certainly know your stuff."

"You could do the same if it wasn't so personal," she responded. "I know from experience how difficult it truly is."

"Lunch time," Hazel announced, popping her head around the study door. "It is set up in the kitchen, so don't argue. You both need a break, I'm certain."

Nathan glanced across at Grace. How much had Hazel heard, she wondered. Luckily, they weren't talking about the missing money. It was something Nathan had insisted they keep from her. Grace was certain he was doing the right thing. Hazel had been through a lot lately, losing her husband like that and didn't need any extra worry.

Grace knew what a shock loss could be. She was still trying to get over Kate's death and wondered if she ever would.

Chapter Fourteen

"Thank you, Mother," Nathan said, glancing up at his mother. "We'll only be a minute. We just need to finish what we're doing here." He pointed to the screen, and she smiled.

"Don't be too long, dear. The food will go cold."

Knowing his mother, she would have gone to a lot of trouble, so they mustn't be long. Hazel had always loved to cook and spent much of her time in the kitchen. So much so, Jonathan Ayes had purchased a bespoke kitchen to ensure Hazel had the kitchen that was perfect for her needs.

"Done. Now, to get the figures in real time, you need to click this button," Grace told him.

Nathan continued to watch over her shoulder and watched as the daily takings so far today, rolled across the screen. "Technology truly is amazing," he said.

"I already checked, and your accounting package is compatible with this software." She glanced up at him. "That said, at this point in time, it's not really what we want. Let's get a clearer picture before transferring the information." Grace lowered her voice for the last two sentences.

Since Nathan had insisted, she'd created a secure logon for the computer. Not that he expected anyone else to try and access their records, but it was an additional security check. She closed it down and they hurried out for lunch.

"This is delicious, Hazel," Grace said, and Nathan knew she was stating facts. His mother was the best cook he'd ever come across.

Hazel waved a hand in the air. "Goodness, Grace," she said. "It's only homemade vegetable soup. Nothing fancy."

"It's very special to me," Grace insisted, giving a wry smile. "I've been living on tv dinners lately."

Heat rose in her cheeks, and Nathan knew she felt embarrassed about having revealed such a personal detail. Her eyes immediately went to the soup sitting in front of her. "Have some bread," Nathan told her, trying to change the subject and take the focus from her. "I'll bet Mother made this, too."

"I did, dear. Sourdough bread. It's good for us." She pushed the board with the bread toward Nathan. "Cut some more will you, Nathan?" she asked.

He reached across and sliced more bread. Nathan placed it on a plate, pushing the bread and butter toward Grace. "We've been working hard, Mother," Nathan said. "I don't know what we would do without Grace."

"We should have her here permanently. It makes perfect sense to me." Nathan was shocked at his mother's words. "You know how much time your father spent in that blasted study. It was too much." She shook her head then. "Water under the bridge, now." Hazel sighed.

Nathan knew exactly what she was saying. His father had spent his last months at the computer. Only now did he know the reason why. He had no intention of telling his mother – she had more than enough stress to deal with as it was.

"Why don't we talk about this later, Mother. Let Grace enjoy her meal." Yes, he was trying to deflect. Nathan knew his mother well. She would eventually get around to asking exactly what it was they were doing. Of course, the answer would be installing software.

They all went quiet, and you could hear a pin drop. The three concentrated on eating instead of talking, which suited Nathan fine. He didn't want to talk business to his mother. She was not a businesswoman, and never had been. Jonathan Ayes was old school. In the early days of taking over the business, she helped out here and there. But mostly she ran the household.

Because that's what wives did back then. Once Nathan was born, she never again had anything to do with running the tree farm. She was not even considered a silent partner, and from what Nathan could tell, Hazel was happy for it to be that way.

His father's will was very concise – everything went to Nathan. His mother was to be cared for and live in the homestead for the rest of her life, if that was what she wanted. There was no question. Of course, Nathan would ensure his mother was well looked after and always have a home here.

Why Father had left everything to Nathan, he wasn't sure. Perhaps it was his way of forcing is son to move back to Blue Ridge permanently. Nathan would never know for certain now.

Grace suddenly stood and began to collect up the soiled dishes.

"No, Grace. That's my job," Hazel told her.

Frowning, Grace continued on her quest. "I am quite capable of helping," she said gently.

Hazel went to her side and took over. "Not on my watch," she said.

Grace shrugged her shoulders. "Hazel is a force to be reckoned with," she told Nathan. He couldn't help but laugh.

"She is," he said. "Honestly though, let her have her way. It's what makes her happy."

"If that's what you think I should do, I will." It was easy to see Grace had always been a hard worker. The simple task of cleaning up seemed to be a necessity for her. It seemed no matter if it was work or pleasure, she always did her best.

"It's exactly what I believe you should do. Let us pamper you for a change." The expression on her face was priceless. Had she never been cared for? Or even pampered in her life?

"Exactly," Hazel said, as she carried a tray of bowls.

"You should have let me carry those, Mother," Nathan said.

"You worry too much," Hazel admonished him. "It's not heavy." After placing the soiled dishes in the sink, she put a bowl of apple crumble and custard in front of each person, then sat down. "Eat up, before it gets cold."

He watched as Grace took a mouthful. She closed her eyes, and it was clear from her expression she savored the taste. "This is delicious, Hazel. You're an amazing cook."

His mother laughed. "You're simply not used to homemade cooking. I'm a pretty ordinary cook, to tell the truth."

"I really doubt that," Grace told his mother. "I wish I could cook. I can barely boil an egg."

Nathan heard his mother gasp. "My dear girl," she said gently. "That needs to change, and quickly. Perhaps I can teach you some time?"

The thought of having Grace at the homestead more often sent warmth through Nathan's body. He wasn't sure what it was about her, but having Grace around had been one of the highlights of his entire life.

Chapter Fifteen

Grace knew Hazel was right. She rarely cooked for herself – it wasn't something she was comfortable doing. More often than not, she zapped a tv dinner in the microwave. Those things were fine now and then, but she had made a habit of having them most nights.

It wasn't good for her health. Nor was it good for her mental wellbeing. It had become worse since... Grace didn't want to think about her loss. She was trying to be more positive.

She sat in front of the computer and watched the sales rolling in. Nathan sat beside her. "I like this," he said with a grin. "I've never seen such a thing before. You, Grace Devlin, are a miracle worker."

Grace could take that sort of praise all day, except nothing she'd done was exceptional. It was her job. "I'm willing to bet those figures will skyrocket once the new register is delivered and installed."

"I'm so excited for it to arrive tomorrow," Nathan said with enthusiasm.

"If it arrives tomorrow." Grace wasn't convinced. The snow was good for the Ayes' business, but not for big trucks making deliveries.

Nathan pulled out his cell phone and checked the weather map. "Moderate snow is predicted for tomorrow," he said. "Hopefully, that means it will be delivered as planned."

Grace hoped so, too. Setting the new compatible register up shouldn't be difficult. The hardest part of the process would be getting Melody used to it. The tree farm cash register was quite old. The more modern registers had far more options. She aired her concerns to Nathan.

He thought about it for a few minutes. "We could pull someone from the gift shop to teach her," he finally said. "If I knew how, I'd do it, but I know nothing about those registers. Nor do I have a clue how each arm of the business operates."

Grace was shocked. She understood Nathan had been back in Blue Ridge for around five months, maybe six. Although she was aware he'd been helping his father with the business side of things. Mostly to do with ensuring everything would continue to run smoothly once Jonathan Ayes passed. "Perhaps it's time," Grace said gently. "Your father knew everything about his business. He knew every staff member by sight and could step in at any time should he be needed."

Nathan turned to face her. "You're right. I should do the same before it gets too busy." He glanced down at his watch. "It's not too late today. Besides, I need to speak to Damian about borrowing one of his gift shop staff to train Melody tomorrow."

"Perhaps you can step into that person's job for the duration." Grace was being bold, but she was, after all, being paid to sort out the problems the business was facing. That didn't mean she was restricted to only the accounting. If it did, she would have been home hours ago.

Nathan grinned again. She loved when he was happy. "That's a brilliant idea," he said. "Do you feel like another stroll?"

"Always," Grace said. "Especially here. The air is crisp and clean, and it's so peaceful. I could easily live out here."

"Hardwick Falls is quiet, too, isn't it?" he asked.

"Most of the time, but not as serene as it is here. You can hear yourself think, as well as the birds tittering in the trees."

"Are we converting you from a city gal to a country one?" Nathan joked.

It made Grace laugh. "Not a city gal. Never that. Hardwick Falls is more like a village. Many of the residents know each other. People know most of the dog's names, but not necessarily their owner's names." She laughed again. Grace couldn't help it. "I'm still learning," she said conspiratorially. "Being such a recent dog owner," she added.

"Of course," Nathan told her.

Grace glanced about. "It's still busy. Even while it's snowing." She was incredulous. In her mind, Grace believed customers would stay away while it snowed.

"The tree farm is busiest when it's snowing," Nathan told her.

They continued their stroll until they eventually reached Melody and her sales area. "Melody," Nathan called since she had her back to them.

She spun around, and they could see she was shivering. Nathan frowned. So did Grace. "I wanted to let you know we've ordered a new cash register for this department," Nathan said. "Why are you so cold?"

It was then Grace glanced about. The wooden sides of the kiosk Melody worked in had fallen off and sat nearby. The roof was also in a state of disrepair. Even if it had been in good condition, the kiosk was far too small. "Nathan," Grace said, pulling on his sleeve. "Look at the condition of this *building*. No wonder Melody is shivering."

He stared at the open walls, and the roof with its gaps. "This won't do," Nathan said firmly. "Why didn't I notice this before?" It was clear from his tone Nathan was annoyed with himself.

"The wooden sides fell off a short time ago. It wasn't too bad while they were still intact," Melody told him, with no malice in her voice.

"From now on," Nathan said firmly, "any problems, you come straight to me. This needs to be fixed immediately." He spotted one of the workers who helped with the trees and directed the man to follow him. "We need to rebuild this kiosk, only better than it is now. Much bigger," Nathan told him. "Are you up for it?"

"Yes, Sir, Mr. Ayes," the man said. "I'm Jason, by the way."

Nathan studied him. "It's Nathan. Mr. Ayes was my father." The two men walked away together, chatting about what needed to be done.

Grace felt at a loss. Nathan had clearly forgotten about her in his quest to fix a problem that should never have occurred.

"Melody," she said as the young woman stared after the two men. "Nathan didn't finish telling you his plans. I can do that." Melody seemed very open to the changes, which was impressive. The cash register appeared ancient and had probably been in use since day one.

"It looks like things are changing for the better," Melody said.

Grace agreed. "I couldn't agree more," she said, then headed back to the homestead.

Chapter Sixteen

Nathan scrounged through the workshop next to the homestead. He was almost certain his father had a pile of good timber in there. He and Jason discussed what was needed for the kiosk to keep Melody and other staff safe, warm, and comfortable.

They were lucky the whole thing hadn't collapsed while customers were there. Or harmed any staff. The business could have been sued if anyone was injured. Nathan knew part of the issue was the missing money. His mind was elsewhere lately. Trying to find the person who was embezzling money from the business.

Grace had found the thefts, but he still couldn't believe his father refused to allow her to investigate. If only Father had documented his suspicions. It would make it so much easier. There was only one reason for that – Jonathan Ayes knew the culprit and was covering up for them. But why would he?

As far as Nathan was concerned, if a worker was stealing from the business, they needed to go to jail. There was no other option.

"I found some decent timber up here," Jason yelled from the loft. "I think there's enough for what you need to do. Is there a toolbox down there? I can't see one up here."

Jason was older than Nathan expected any of the workers to be. He was probably in his mid to late fifties, and wondered why the worker chose a seasonal job, and not something permanent. He scrounged around. "I found the toolbox," he said. "Along with some power tools. Now we need to get the timber down here."

They spent the next fifteen minutes taking the timber down piece by piece. It was in good condition, possibly brand new, and would work well for what they needed.

"We could do most of the work here in the workshop," Jason told him. "Then put it together onsite."

"That's a wonderful idea," Nathan told him. "This is what I have in mind." He reached for a pencil, then did a rough drawing on a wooden bench.

Jason studied it for a few minutes. He took the pencil from Nathan. "What if you change it to include some additional features? I've worked in that kiosk, and know the current one is inadequate." He made some subtle changes then added a cupboard and small window on two sides. "I would also make the kiosk lockable. It currently has no door and is open to vandalism as it is now." He turned to Nathan for his opinion. "It's not been vandalized to date, as far as

I'm aware, but the world is sadly changing," he added.

Nathan was impressed. He valued this man's input and told him so. "Those ideas are wonderful, Jason. You clearly have experience in this area."

The other man shrugged. "I'm a carpenter by trade. Worked as a handyman for a few years. This job is a breeze," he said, then chuckled.

Nathan was astounded. "You are exactly what I need. I will pay you carpentry rates for this job," he said. "No argument. I am very concerned for Melody and anyone else using the current kiosk." He glanced at his watch. "It's too late to finish it today."

"We can get a good start on it," Jason insisted. He glanced at the drawing again, running his fingers over the lines, as though memorizing them. "We've got around two hours left today. I can come in early tomorrow if that helps. We could have it done by lunchtime at the latest."

Jason was keen if nothing else, and that impressed Nathan. Perhaps he could find other jobs around the place for Jason to do. He was clearly far too qualified to be chopping down trees.

If the kiosk was in such a poor state, it made Nathan wonder about the rest of the place. "Tea or coffee, Jason?" Nathan asked.

The other man stared at him. "I'd rather work on this project," he said.

"Let's do both," Nathan replied.

~*~

"It's so nice to see men using this workshop again," Hazel said as she delivered coffee and cake to the two men. "I've missed those days."

"Thank you, Mrs. Ayes," Jason said, as he reached for a mug.

Nathan could see he was itching to keep working on this project. It made him wonder about other projects he could find for Jason. He was far too skilled to be merely cutting down Christmas trees. "You're too young to be retired," Nathan said, hoping Jason might open up a little. It would help him decide what to do going forward.

Jason took a long sip of his coffee before answering. "Along with several other highly skilled workers, I was made redundant a couple of years ago. I've been taking on jobs here and there as they came available."

"Like chopping down trees," Nathan said.

"Mostly handyman stuff, but a few carpentry jobs here and there. Nothing like this, though. I enjoy the challenge."

"But not the money? It surely isn't as good as what you were earning." Nathan was almost certain on that point.

Jason studied him before answering. "Along with the others, I received a decent redundancy package. I paid off my house, and still had plenty to live on. Staying home all the time gets boring, so I keep an eye out for anything that piques my interest."

Nathan frowned. Surely using an axe to cut down pine trees was not interesting. It would have to get boring waiting for customers to need assistance. "And this job interested you?" Nathan found it hard to believe.

"I'll be truthful – it didn't interest me at all but would keep me busy for the month."

"What if you found something permanent? Would that interest you?" Nathan wasn't promising anything, or even offering. He was simply trying to understand Jason's situation.

Jason stared at him. "Beyond December, do you mean?"

"Perhaps. I'm not promising anything. Just asking for now." Nathan finished his coffee, and the conversation returned to the project at hand. It was the most important task right now.

Tomorrow, weather permitting, the new cash register would arrive. It would need protection, so having the new kiosk finished and installed well before it was delivered was the aim.

The two men worked well together. Jason took the lead, since he was the experienced carpenter, and

Nathan followed his instructions. It was an enjoyable afternoon.

Except for the fact he missed Grace. What was that about?

Chapter Seventeen

Melody was excited about the new equipment, but more so for the new kiosk. As a new employee, she didn't want to jeopardize her job by complaining about the state of dilapidation the current kiosk was in. Especially since it was seasonal and wouldn't last long.

"Nathan is not like that," Grace had told her. "He's working toward improvements and is clearly upset you've endured such conditions."

"I can see that now," Melody said, pulling her coat tighter around herself.

Before she left, Grace offered to cover for Melody so she could take a break. She quickly showed Grace how to use the register and the credit card facility, although both were quite basic. "Thank you," Melody said excitedly, then disappeared toward the café.

Another twenty-four hours or so, and not only should the new equipment arrive, but hopefully, the new kiosk would be finished. Grace didn't know much about such things, but it seemed a small project. Or at least, smallish. Surely it wouldn't take that long?

It didn't feel long before Melody returned. "I really appreciate having that break," she said. "I hope I wasn't gone too long."

"It didn't seem long enough," Grace said. "Are you sure you've had enough time?"

The young woman didn't hesitate. "It's plenty. I truly do appreciate it."

They said their goodbyes, and Grace headed back to the homestead.

The moment she arrived, she checked on Penny, who was still in her bed, snuggled up with Arnie. The two were so sweet together. It was clear to Grace, they needed each other. They were both grieving, even if Arnie had not known Jonathan very long before he passed. Dogs were very sensitive in that way. Not to mention he would sense Hazel and Nathan were also grieving.

Knowing the dogs were fine, she headed toward the kitchen to let Hazel know she was back.

"I was just making myself a drink," Hazel said. "Would you like one?" She shook herself then. "Of course you would. You've been out in that awful weather." Before Grace even had a chance to answer, a mug of coffee was placed in front of her.

"You know I can do that for myself, right?" Grace said. "You are not my maid, or my slave."

Hazel shook her head. "It's the one thing I'm good at. Jonathan always said I was no good in the business, but I shine in the kitchen. He was right. They were his exact words," she said, her gaze now in far off places.

"He was a good man," Hazel told her. "It was all too much in the end. I begged him to stop. He almost did when..." She suddenly stopped speaking, and the color drained from her face.

Grace wondered what Hazel was about to divulge. Should she tell Nathan what his mother had said?

She hated to come between mother and son, but this could be a clue to helping them find the culprit.

Grace wanted to ask Hazel for more information, but she appeared devastated at what she'd already revealed. The last thing Grace wanted was to upset Hazel. She'd been so kind to Grace, and to Penny. Not to mention she was still grieving the loss of her husband of almost half a century.

"It's so peaceful out here," Grace said, trying to fill the silence Hazel's words had caused. "Apart from the cold, I could live here." Hazel studied her. "I do love Hardwick Falls," Grace added, "but Blue Ridge is even better."

Hazel smiled. "I can't help but agree. You and Nathan go well together," she added.

Was Hazel trying to match her and Nathan? They got on well together, and Grace enjoyed his company.

The time she'd spent with Nathan had been some of the best days she'd had for months. "We are teaching each other," Grace told her. "I'm teaching him a few accounting things, and he's teaching me the bigger picture of the business."

Hazel raised her eyebrows. "And now he's out in the workshop with Jason someone, building a new kiosk." She chuckled then. "Nathan used to build things with his dad, until he moved to the city. That was a sad day for us all."

"I can only imagine," Grace said.

"It had to happen, I know it did. He wanted to do a business course. There's nothing like that around here."

"I had to do the same thing," Grace said quietly. "It was a difficult decision, as I'm sure it was for Nathan."

Hazel appeared thoughtful and took a long sip of her drink. "I never thought of it that way," she said, then placed her mug on the table. "I didn't even offer you a cookie," she said, sounding anxious. Hazel pushed her chair back, but Grace stopped her.

"Please don't on my account," she said. "I have done nothing but eat since I arrived." She grinned then, and the two women laughed.

The camaraderie between them was heartfelt, but Grace knew the questions she had about missing money may jeopardize it. Nothing she did or said could stop it. Thousands of dollars were missing from the business. At best it was illegal. At worst, the business was out far more than forty thousand dollars.

Money that must be recovered for the Ayes family business to survive another holiday season.

~*~

Grace sat in front of the computer and studied the figures coming through. She should have looked into this a long time ago. Jonathan would have appreciated seeing sales in real time. She felt certain this technology would have been available back then.

Nothing she could do about it now. It was in the past, and she needed to look toward the future. Not only for herself, but for her client. Funny, but Nathan didn't feel like a client. He felt more like a friend – one she'd known for many years.

It was strange. Grace had always kept to herself for as long as she could remember. Her laptop had been the barrier she put between herself and everyone else. She'd rejected Kate's pleas for her to get another cat after losing her precious ginger cat, Shadow because at least that way she would have company. She didn't want a dog either, but no way was Grace allowing Penny to be dumped in a shelter.

It's what Kate's lawyer wanted to do. Grace was having none of it. She had fumbled her way through learning to care for an elderly dog, but finally worked it out with the help of the internet. As she did with most other challenges in her life.

Grace glanced up as she heard someone enter the study. "Nathan," she said more cheerfully than she'd anticipated. "I think Hazel knows something about the missing money," she said carefully.

He frowned. "You told her?"

She flinched at the annoyance on his face and in his voice. "No, I didn't. She told me. At least I think that's what she did."

His annoyance turned to shock.

Chapter Eighteen

Nathan put a finger to his lips. "Not another word," he whispered, right before he snatched up Grace's coat and scarf. "I am excited to show you what Jason and I have done so far," he said, his voice at a normal level.

He hoped Grace understood he didn't want to discuss the missing money in case his mother overheard.

The moment they were outside and out of range of the house, Grace turned to him. "What's going on?" she asked, sounding more than a little frustrated.

"If you didn't tell Mother about the missing money, and I certainly didn't, how did she find out?" He raised his eyebrows, then grabbed Grace by the hand and dragged her into the workshop. "What do you think?" he asked as they approached the partially made kiosk.

"It is beautiful. Melody will be so pleased." Grace ran her fingers along the side. "The poor girl told me she was too scared to tell you the current kiosk was falling apart."

That upset him. Nathan thought he was approachable, and didn't expect to hear this. "I hope you put her straight," he told her.

"She also rarely gets a break," she told him, ignoring his last comment. "I manned the kiosk for her so she could have one. Seriously, Nathan, you need to look into this. Apart from the fact there are laws about such things, you need to look after your staff better than this."

Grace looked annoyed. As she should be. He was on the verge of anger – at himself. He'd wasted too much time on unimportant tasks and ignored the significant ones. "We plan to have the kiosk finished by noon tomorrow. We are making it in parts and will assemble it on the site."

"It sounds like a plan," Grace told him. "I received a text stating the new register is loaded on the truck and weather permitting, will be delivered tomorrow afternoon."

Nathan let out a long breath. "That's cutting it fine, but Jason is coming in early tomorrow so we can get a good start. I discovered he's a carpenter," Nathan added.

"What are the chances?" Grace said matter-of-factly. "Now, about what Hazel said…"

Nathan stared at her. Did he really want to go there? "I was totally unaware my mother knew money had disappeared." He sighed then. Did he really want to know? Except Nathan knew it had to come out. "All I can think is Father told her."

"She didn't exactly say she knew about the missing money," Grace said firmly. "It was more of an inference. Hazel told me she begged your father to stop. I took that to mean stop working. Or perhaps close down the business."

She studied him then. Closely, and it made Nathan uncomfortable. "What does it even mean?" Did it mean his mother knew someone was stealing from the company business? Or was it simply an assumption on her part?

"I honestly don't know," she said gently. "But we have to explore all possibilities."

Nathan knew Grace was right. They had to follow through and not assume anything. Once the new register was installed, it would be far easier to clear things up.

If his mother did know who stole the money, why hadn't she told him? The tree farm had survived generations but was on the verge of collapse because some unknown person had been stealing from them.

Before he could say another word, the door to the workshop flew open. "Oh my, it's cold out there," Hazel said as she hurried inside. "Supper is ready. Will you be long?" She glanced at the project Nathan and Jason had been working on. "It looks lovely. I'm sure it's better than that old kiosk. It's been there almost since the beginning."

No wonder it was on its last legs. "That stops tomorrow," Nathan said firmly. "We need to look out for our staff. Did you know they're not getting proper breaks?" His heart hammered wondering what his mother would say about it.

"Oh, Nathan," she said, annoyance in her tone. "You know very well I don't get involved in the business." With that, she turned and headed back outside. "Don't be long. The food will go cold," she said over her shoulder.

The moment Hazel closed the door, he turned to Grace, who was staring at the door his mother had effectively slammed. "What just happened?" he asked Grace, feeling quite perplexed.

"I really don't know," Grace answered. "But I do believe Hazel knows more than she's letting on. I suggest you carry out the plans you've already made and see what happens over the next week or so."

Grace was right. They needed more proof, and the only way to get it was with patience.

~*~

"I'm so glad you are replacing that old kiosk," Hazel said out of the blue. "This time of the year it's far too cold for anyone to endure the weather." She visibly shook then, as though she was physically out in the cold.

Grace reached for her cell phone. "I just had an idea," she said, then ran a search. "Should we be supplying a freezer jacket? Like they use in commercial freezers?"

Nathan chuckled at her use of the term 'we'. Strangely enough, she did feel like part of the business. Not to mention the family. Grace had suggested changes he would never have thought about and was knowledgeable in many areas. "It's certainly something to think about," he said. "I guess they are pricey?"

"Not as much as you'd think. A couple of hundred dollars." Grace glanced up from her phone to study him. His mind went back to her earlier words about looking after staff.

"Let's discuss it further after supper," he said, then glanced across at his mother. She had never agreed with business talk at the table. "The meal is delicious, Mother," he said with a smile.

"It is, Hazel. I wish I could cook. I can't even make the most basic of meals." Grace sighed then. It had become clear to Nathan she was more interested in her accounting business than in her private life, or looking after herself for that matter.

Hazel waved both their compliments aside. "It's roast chicken for goodness' sake," she said. "Nothing to write home about. Mind you, the dessert is another thing altogether."

His mother was teasing them, Nathan knew. She was an excellent cook and always had been.

"If you're interested, I could teach you, Grace," Hazel said out of the blue.

Her words told Nathan she'd taken a liking to the woman who ensured their accounting was up to date and accurate.

"That sounds wonderful," Grace said. "Sadly, I don't have time at the moment. I must get your books sorted."

Hazel rolled her eyes. "Business talk again," she said, then went back to her meal.

Chapter Nineteen

Grace should not have brought up business at the table. She knew better than that. Although the dining room seemed more casual than formal, Hazel set the table as though it was the latter.

She was old school, and there was no getting away from it. The meals she served were better than any restaurant meal Grace had ever had, and she could easily get used to them.

"Cream?" Hazel asked as she placed a large piece of apple pie in front of Grace.

"Thank you," Grace said. "It looks and smells delicious."

"It's nothing special, dear. You're simply not used to homemade food."

Grace leaned in closer. The aroma drew her in. She couldn't remember such an amazing scent before. Out of the corner of her eye, she noticed Nathan staring. "What?" she asked. "I've not had homemade pie for a very long time.

"Take a mouthful," Nathan said, so she did.

All eyes were on her, and the silence was palpable. "Mmmm, this is amazing," she declared.

Hazel grinned. "Of course it is."

Nathan laughed, and Hazel began to eat her own dessert. "Apple pie is one of the easiest desserts to make," she said between mouthfuls. "I'll have to teach you," she added.

It sounded good to Grace, and she said so.

Later that night, sitting next to Nathan on the sofa in the lounge room, Grace felt part of this family. Penny was content curled up on her lap, and Arnie seemed happy curled up on Hazel's. She watched the snow falling outside as the three of them sat inside where a woodfire was burning. Never did she feel so much at home. Like she belonged here.

Everyone said she was strange. Quirky even. Grace didn't feel that way. She wasn't a people person, never had been. She was more comfortable alone, or with her pets. They didn't judge her. Instead, they gave Grace unconditional love.

Jonathan had accepted her for who she was, and it seemed Nathan and Hazel were the same. Perhaps it was the reason she felt so comfortable here.

Nathan reached out and petted Penny. "She's a good dog," he said as he continued to stroke Penny's head. "It must have been quite a shock when you suddenly had to take her."

She turned to face him. "It was at first. My sister's lawyer wanted to send her to a shelter. I couldn't allow that," she said quietly. "Kate would have hated it." She leaned in and put her cheek against Penny's head. "Penny is a senior and deserves better than that. Besides, I think Kate would have haunted me forever more."

Nathan chuckled. Grace joined him. It felt good to laugh. She needed the release. Life had been tense lately, but coming here had been the best thing she'd done in ages. Nathan slid his hand across to hers. Grace stared down at their entwined hands but said nothing.

Penny's head shot up, then she barked. "I think she wants to go potty," Grace said, scooping the dog up into her arms.

"Nathan, perhaps you can take Arnie out, too." Hazel was already standing and passing the pup over to him.

"Good idea," he said. "I guess it's getting late. I have an early start tomorrow. Jason is coming around eight so we can get a head start on the kiosk. I don't want Melody using it for even one more day."

"I don't suppose you have a smallish tent you could put up for now? Pull the rest of the old kiosk down and use the tent temporarily?" Grace was thinking out loud. She didn't mean to announce it to all and sundry. It was meant to be an idea to toss around in her mind.

"It's an excellent idea," Nathan said as they walked outside together, each carrying a dog. I believe we may have an old tent, but not sure how big it is. Or what sort of condition it's in."

"We can sort it out in the morning," Grace said. "It was just an idea."

Nathan frowned, and she wondered if she had offended him. "It's a good idea. I'll be up early to get to work on the new kiosk. The last thing I want is for Melody to be exposed to the elements."

After the dogs went potty, they went back into the house. Hazel announced she was retiring for the evening. Grace bid her goodnight, then turned to Nathan. He seemed somewhat sad. "Are you alright?" she asked gently.

He seemed to perk up a little. "Seeing all these changes are a little hard to swallow. Except I know they are needed. Many of them should have been done long ago." He petted Arnie, then reached out to Penny. "I collected the three bags of cash, checked them, and placed them in the safe. Everything seems to be as it should," he whispered, not wanting Hazel to overhear their conversation.

Nathan knew how much money talk upset his mother, so tried to hide the harsh realities of the business from her.

"Fingers crossed the cash tallies up with the receipts," Grace said.

"They do," Nathan told her quietly. "I checked. Everything aligns perfectly at this point."

"That's good. We can only hope it continues. Finding the thief is the one thing we must do. It's my mission to solve the mystery," Grace told him. "Now, it's time for sleep. It's been an exhausting day."

"Goodnight, Grace. Goodnight, Penny," he said, giving the dog a final pet. "I'll see you in the morning."

Moments later he was gone.

Grace placed Penny in her bed, which she'd moved earlier. She prepared for bed, then glanced out the window. The winter wonderland happening outside brought back memories. Too many from days gone by.

Memories that should be comforting, but with the loss of her sister so raw, they were far from soothing.

Penny was already curled up and appeared to be asleep. Grace climbed into bed and turned off the light.

Tomorrow was another day and would bring its own set of challenges.

Chapter Twenty

Nathan was up bright and early.

The house was quiet. He was determined to dismantle the remainder of the dilapidated kiosk. He remembered where the tent was and took it with him. It wasn't huge, but since it was only a temporary fix, it would do the job.

He glanced down at his watch. Jason was arriving at eight, which meant he had around thirty minutes to get everything done.

"You started without me." Jason's voice pierced the icy air.

Nathan had never felt so relieved. "I want to get this dangerous structure down. I should have done it yesterday."

Jason didn't wait to be asked, he immediately helped with the task. "Is that a tent?" he asked, staring at the pile of canvas on the ground.

"A temporary fix until the new kiosk is ready."

Jason slapped him on the back. "Good to see you are looking out for Melody. She is a good worker, and a good person."

Nathan couldn't help but agree.

With the old structure gone, and the tent now standing, they were ready to leave. They carried as much of the old timber as they could, then dumped it in the workshop. "Time for coffee," Nathan said. "That's cold work. How do you stand it all day?" he asked.

Jason studied him. "Some days it is unbelievably cold. Unbearable even. There have been times we've all huddled in the kiosk with Melody."

Nathan was appalled. How could he be so unaware of what his employees were dealing with? "This stops now! Changes are happening," he explained. "Grace found freezer jackets online. They should help."

"That woman is worth her weight in gold," Jason said, as they entered the homestead.

Nathan was surprised to find Grace and Hazel sitting in the kitchen. "Good morning," he told them. "This is Jason. He's an amazing carpenter. This is Grace, our accountant, and Hazel, my mother."

They all shook hands, and Hazel poured coffee for the men. "I was about to make breakfast," Hazel said. "Sit down. It won't be long."

"We need to start on the kiosk," Nathan argued.

Hazel put her hands to her hips. "Breakfast is the most important meal of the day. The kiosk can wait a few more minutes."

It wasn't long before they were all sitting around the kitchen table with bacon and eggs, and a side of toast. Nathan was certain Jason didn't know what hit him.

~*~

"Mrs. Ayes," Jason said, "this is the best breakfast I've ever had."

Nathan sensed he wasn't just saying it to be polite. He seemed genuine. "Thank you for including me."

Hazel stared at him. "If that's the best breakfast you've had, I can see why you are so skinny," she said matter-of-factly.

Everyone laughed, including Jason.

"Nah," he said. "It's hard work. I've always done manual work. Been a carpenter most of my life," he told her. "Speaking of which, it's time I got started on the kiosk. We're aiming for it to be finished and installed by noon."

Nathan glanced at his watch then stood. "We might just scrape in," he said.

"I've had a text – the delivery is scheduled for around two," Grace said. "That gives you a bit of breathing space." She also stood, then began to gather up the dishes before Hazel could stop her.

A soft bark had them all facing the doorway. Penny had made her way to the sounds she loved best – people. It wasn't long before Arnie followed her in, and made his mark by barking, too.

"I can take care of them both," Nathan said, and reached for their leads.

Grace mouthed *thank you*, and warmth filled him. "This will only take a minute," he told Jason. Both men rugged up in their thick winter coats.

"You're doing a good thing, both of you," Grace told Jason. Nathan caught her words as he hurried out with the dogs.

Her words filled him with pride. Not because of what she said, although in a way it was. Her words acknowledged he was finally doing the right thing by his employees. It upset Nathan to realize he'd not taken enough time to see what they were enduring. Although to be fair, Melody's position was seasonal, and she'd only been working there a little over a week.

He wondered what her plans were for after the holidays. Was there a position she could fill? Did she even want to continue working for him? It was a question he hadn't contemplated before. Grace had somehow changed his mind set to stop thinking about the business and start considering the people who made it work. *His loyal workers.*

The moment he was back inside and settled the dogs, he and Jason hurried out to the workshop. Jason went straight to work. He didn't so much as ask Nathan what he wanted him to do. He was the ultimate professional, and someone Nathan wanted on his team. "What are you doing after the holidays?" Nathan asked as Jason cut the timber to size.

Jason glanced up momentarily. "No plans at this point," he said. "Like I told you, I look for seasonal jobs then move on."

"Is that because you want to, or because you have to?" Nathan demanded. How anyone could not recognize Jason's skills was beyond him.

Jason stopped what he was doing and stood tall. "Mostly out of necessity. After I was retrenched, I was considered too old. I am fifty-six years old," he said with disgust in his voice. "Moving from job to job was my only option."

"How would you feel if I offered you a permanent job?" Nathan asked. "As carpenter and handyman? There is so much that needs fixing around here, and I'm not particularly good with my hands. I'm far better with the business side of things," he said.

"I've noticed," Jason said with a chuckle. "I would love to take you up on your offer. I can't thank you enough." He reached over and shook Nathan's hand.

"Welcome to the team, and your private domain," Nathan said indicating the workshop, then they both went back to work.

Chapter Twenty-One

Grace retired to the study once she'd helped Hazel with the breakfast dishes.

"You should stay, dear," Hazel said. "I can teach you how to cook."

As much as she'd like to stay, Grace couldn't. "I am truly sorry," she said. "I have work to do. It's what Nathan is paying me for."

"Fair enough," Hazel said. "Another time perhaps."

"I would love that," Grace said before hurrying out of the kitchen.

Penny was already settled in the study and seemed pleased to see her. Grace was more than happy to see Penny. They were best friends now. When she first brought Penny into her home, the dog was unable to settle. That's when she moved into Kate's house.

The strange thing was, Penny was quite at home here. It wasn't like she'd been there before, because she hadn't. Before this week, she'd been coming out alone. Penny was not part of Grace's life then, except when she visited her sister at home or the florist shop.

Her life had certainly changed since getting Penny. For the better.

She typed in her security password for the computer and opened the file that told her what sales had occurred that day. In a few short hours, the delivery should arrive. She would then set it up to send reports to the computer.

For Grace, it was exciting watching all those numbers scroll down the screen. She could only imagine how it made Nathan feel.

She reached for the printed statements she'd locked in a drawer of the desk. It was quite complexing. There was no rhyme or reason to the thefts. Just random amounts disappearing. Grace shook herself mentally. She needed to stop thinking and start working.

Nathan and Jason were busy working on the new kiosk, and she had her designated tasks to carry out. First on the list was freezer wear for Melody and the men tasked with cutting down the trees. First though, she needed their sizes.

Somehow her position as accountant had morphed into something completely different. For once in her life, Grace didn't mind at all.

There was a time she would have refused, but here with Nathan, she was happy to do whatever was needed to get the business running smoothly.

~*~

Lunch was over, and Grace had been sitting in front of the computer for far too long today. Stretching her back and neck, Grace decided she needed to walk. Sitting for hours on end was not good for anyone. She had been crunching numbers and updating spreadsheets. It was her favorite thing to do, although many people questioned that about her.

She pulled on her thick coat and scarf, then hurried to the kitchen to let Hazel know she was off for a walk. Except Hazel wasn't there. She couldn't see Arnie either. Grace checked the other rooms in the house. She finally found Hazel and Arnie in the dining room. What she saw there shocked her.

Grace quietly doubled back and collected Penny, then after waiting a sufficient amount of time, went into the dining room again, talking to Penny as she did so. "Oh, there you are Hazel," she said. "I'm going for a stroll. Would you like to come?" she offered, knowing full well Hazel did not like the cold.

Hazel reached out and petted Arnie, who was sitting on her lap. "I'm fine, dear. I like to avoid snow when I can." She smiled then, but her smile didn't seem natural. Hazel appeared nervous, and Grace was certain she knew why.

"Oh," Grace said. "That painting seems a little crooked."

Hazel's head snapped up, and she stared at the painting on the wall. "I...I was dusting," she said. "I must have bumped it."

"That must be it," Grace said, then walked over to pet Arnie before they left. "It's a pretty painting," she added.

"It's the original homestead from many years ago," Hazel told her.

Grace studied it. "It is lovely," she said, then said her farewells. She hurried out of the room before she was further distracted.

The closer she got to where the dilapidated kiosk once stood, the more impressed she was. "It's beautiful," she said when she reached the site where the new kiosk now stood. "You two have done a magnificent job," she told Jason and Nathan. "What do you think Melody?"

"It's wonderful," she said. "I cannot thank either of them enough for what they've done."

"Your new register should arrive soon. Once it's here, we have arranged one of the gift shop staff to come and teach you how to use it."

Melody smiled. "That is such a relief," she said. "I was worried I'd have to work it out myself."

"Not this time." Grace glanced up as she heard the sound of an engine. "Speak of the devil," she said. "This will be what we've been waiting for."

The driver pulled in as close to the kiosk as he could get. He confirmed he was in the right place, then removed the register from the truck. He waited while they unpacked it, to ensure there was no damage, then left them.

"It does look modern," Melody said.

Grace laughed. "It better be. It's their latest model. I just have to check the serial number, for the warranty," she said, then wrote the number down. It should be on the paperwork, but better safe than sorry.

By the time Grace was ready to head back to the homestead, Nathan headed out to replace the worker who would teach Melody all the ins and outs of the new equipment.

Any other time, she would be pleased. Grace had news for him, but now it had to wait.

Chapter Twenty-Two

Nathan hurried to the gift shop. This would be a completely different experience for him, but one he was looking forward to. Grace was right – he should know how every aspect of the business worked. It was inexcusable that he didn't know.

Almost the moment Nathan arrived, Peter, from the gift shop, headed toward the kiosk. They greeted each other and then dispersed to where they needed to be. Nathan reported to Damien, who was the gift shop manager.

Damien looked none too pleased, but these were special circumstances. "Good to see you, Nathan," Damien told him despite the scowl on his face. "The shelves need restocking, so I'll get you onto that." He showed Nathan where the storeroom was, and what items needed to be stocked. "If you come across anything else that's low, feel free to fill those as well."

Nathan set about doing what he'd been tasked with. It was quiet in the store, but he knew it wouldn't last. With Christmas almost upon them, the place would soon be buzzing with customers. Many people came only for gifts, and others came for the trees and worked their way to the café and gift shop. Either way, they needed to be accommodated.

It was becoming crystal clear to Nathan that his business degree was totally useless here at the tree farm. He'd worked at a large corporation in the big city for several years, not a small business in a small town. Everything he'd learned had been turned on its head.

There was one other worker in the gift shop. Nathan knew Sharon had worked here for many years. From what he'd been told, she was a good worker, diligent and loyal. He wondered if the staff in the gift shop and café had the same lack of breaks the tree farm staff experienced.

He took the opportunity to speak with her. "Do you get regular breaks?" he asked gently.

"It is difficult at times," Sharon told him. "But we try to work in with each other, so we all get *some* breaks."

He had one more question to ask. "Are you receiving all your legally mandated breaks?" Her face went ashen. "Please be honest with me," Nathan said. "I'm trying to make improvements."

"Rarely," Sharon said, then hurried away before he could grill her further.

So now he knew the truth. The staff were not being treated fairly. This mistreatment had to go back years. Perhaps as far back as when his father took over. It had Nathan wondering if this was the reason for the thefts.

Did someone on the staff believe they were entitled to recompense? Nathan truly hoped it was none of the staff. But if not them, who could it be?

 So far Nathan had not come across anyone who appeared to hold a grudge. Everyone seemed friendly and accommodating, even when he asked difficult questions. He applied himself to the job at hand and followed all the directions he was given.

It was certainly a new experience for him, but Grace was right when she'd told Nathan he needed to understand the business. Since he was now the sole owner of the Ayes Family business, he must ensure it was thriving for any future heirs.

It must have been heartbreaking for his father to learn about the thefts. He went to his grave knowing someone had stolen from him. Even if he had refused to allow Grace to investigate.

In that moment, it struck him like a bolt of lightning. Jonathan Ayes definitely knew who was stealing from them. He had fired Grace to keep that individual's identity a secret.

Peter returned after what seemed like several hours. Nathan found it was a mere ninety minutes when he glanced at his watch. "The new kiosk is great," Peter told Nathan. "Melody is a quick learner. I helped her set up the products – a separate item for each tree size."

For some reason, Nathan felt like a proud father. "Thank you, Peter. You did a great job and I appreciate it." He shook the young man's hand.

Now it was time for Nathan to leave. He still had plenty to do before day's end.

Walking back to the homestead through the snow, even with his thick jacket, Nathan was feeling the cold. He'd deviated to the kiosk to see how Melody liked her new accommodations and the new register. Nathan was satisfied it was far warmer inside the kiosk.

What he did learn was his staff were unnecessarily enduring icy weather. It wasn't snowing heavily today, and already he was shivering. Those working in the tree farm were out in this weather all day. Guilt filled him.

Had his father understood and did nothing? Either way, Nathan had to acknowledge he would be none the wiser if it weren't for Grace pushing him. No matter what, he had to make this right. There was so much he could do to ensure their staff were looked after properly. Not to mention treated in a way they deserved.

Finally reaching the homestead, he saw Grace through the window of the study. Warmth filled him despite the icy temperatures. Standing on the porch, he stared at her for what seemed forever. Until she turned to face him. She smiled and his heart melted.

Hurrying inside, Grace met him at the door. "You must be freezing," she said gently. She was the one person that always made him feel good inside. Even when she was admonishing him for not looking after his staff properly.

"I have something important to tell you," she whispered.

Nathan frowned. Why the secrecy? What could she possibly need to tell him that required her to speak in such a tone he could barely hear her?

"I've learned a lot today," he said as she helped him out of his coat. "Thanks to you."

She studied him, then reached up and brushed some snow from his face. It sent shivers down his spine.

"I've learned a lot today as well," she said. "Totally by accident, and nothing to do with the statistics we've been getting from the registers. Oh, and stats from the new register are already coming through."

Nathan's heart pounded. Not because of the stats, but because something wasn't right. Grace had learned something important.

Something Nathan wasn't sure he was ready to hear.

Chapter Twenty-Three

Heart still pounding, Grace led Nathan into the study and closed the door. Something she rarely did. Nathan sat on the sofa, and Grace sat down close to him. It was going to come as a shock, she was certain and wanted to be nearby in case he needed her.

He studied her closely, but didn't say a word.

Breathing in, then out again, Grace closed her eyes briefly. How she was going to say this, she wasn't sure. "I'm just going to come out and say it," she finally said.

"Please do," he said, interrupting her train of thought. "You have me quite worried."

"As you should be," she said firmly. "Hazel, your mother, was *dusting* this afternoon." It seemed innocent enough but...

"Mother doesn't dust, she has a cleaner who comes in each fortnight."

"Exactly." Not that Grace was aware of the cleaner. "I walked into the loungeroom today and what I saw shocked me enough that I quickly retreated. Before Hazel even knew I'd been there."

"She was dusting?" His voice was full of not only disbelief, but also curiosity.

"The safe was open." She said the words quickly as though saying them might burn her tongue.

"Safe? What safe?" Nathan sounded genuinely surprised about the safe's existence.

"The one behind the painting. That safe." She let her words sink in for a minute or two before continuing. "The door of the safe was wide open, and I could see money in there. Piles of money."

Nathan's eyes opened in surprise. "How much money?" he whispered as though he didn't want to say the words.

"I'm guessing at least the amount missing – forty thousand. Perhaps more." It was then Grace had a thought. "Have you checked yesterday's takings today?"

"That's irrelevant?" Nathan said, although it came out like a question. "You think... Oh no! No, no, no!" he continued. "Mother wouldn't steal from the business."

"Check the takings," she demanded. "Or I will."

It hadn't taken long to confirm what Grace suspected – money was missing from yesterday's takings. Hazel knew the combination to the safe – she'd confirmed it with Nathan. Why, she knew was another thing altogether. Since Hazel had no input into the business, there was no need for her to have access to the study safe.

Nathan wondered if it went way back to when his parents first took over. Mother helped a little until he was born. From that moment on, she was a full-time mother and never helped with the business again.

On opening the safe, it was clear the bags had been disturbed. They sat in different places to where they were placed. Nathan reached in and pulled out all three bags. He opened the first one, which was from the tree farm. His hands were shaking so badly, Grace took over.

The total matched the figure they'd registered as receiving yesterday. It was a relief. The second bag was the gift shop. Five thousand dollars was missing. And three from the café.

Less than twenty-four hours from when the money was received, noted, and placed in the safe, eight thousand dollars had disappeared. Vanished into thin air.

A quick glance at Nathan told Grace all she needed to know. He was devastated, but still didn't want to believe it. Hard and all as it was, he needed to see the proof for himself.

After locking the money bags back in the safe, they headed out to find Hazel. It was a confrontation Grace didn't want to have, but she couldn't let Nathan face his mother alone. "She must have had a good reason," she told him gently. "Although it seems irrelevant now."

"She told you the reason," Nathan said quietly. "She wanted him to stop. I take it to mean stop working. He could have done that, if he'd wanted. Good people work here. I've seen that first hand."

Grace reached for his hand and squeezed it tight. He glanced down into their entwined hands and briefly smiled.

They found Hazel in the very room Grace had discovered her secret. Arnie was curled up on her lap. She glanced up as they walked in and sat down on the sofa opposite.

"Mother," Nathan said gently. "I need to speak with you."

"It's alright, Nathan," she said softly. "I took that money. I'm sorry you had to go through all this work to find out." She glanced across the room at Grace. "I'm also sorry you had to be the one to discover my deception."

Grace was shocked. "You knew? I thought I'd got out of here before you knew I was even there."

Hazel sighed. "I sensed someone there and knew it couldn't be Nathan since he was out there working." She waved toward the window where the snow was falling far heavier than before.

She suddenly lifted Arnie and placed him on the sofa next to her. Without a word, Hazel removed the painting and unlocked the safe. Nathan's eyes opened in astonishment at the mounds of money sitting there.

"It's all there," Hazel said. "I thought if Jonathan believed the business was losing money, he would stop working. He was far too ill to be working anymore."

"He knew it was you," Grace said. "It's the reason he let me go when I discovered the deficit."

"I'm truly sorry, Grace. My actions were not meant to affect you or anyone else."

Except they did. But Grace couldn't tell Hazel that. She was already upset enough. "It's alright, Hazel. I forgive you," she said, then walked over and hugged the older woman. It truly felt like this was the hug they both craved and needed.

"It's alright, Mother," Nathan said. "No harm done. Not really."

It was true. The missing money had been located and retrieved, and the mystery had finally been solved.

Epilogue

Nathan sighed with relief when he and Grace had counted the money from the dining room safe. Every last dollar was accounted for, including the amount that went missing today.

He couldn't understand why his mother had continued to take the money after Jonathan had died. She didn't hesitate when she explained. "I figured I had to keep it up or you'd know something wasn't right," she'd said.

It was obviously correct in her mind.

Grace confirmed all the corrected figures, then carefully entered them into the spreadsheets. Once she was finished, she announced she was ready to leave whenever Nathan could drive her home.

"We still have work to do," he told her. "We have freezer outfits to order, for one. Not just for Melody but for all the outdoor workers. Jackets, pants, and gloves. And anything else you believe is needed." Grace stared at him. "It's cold out there. I found that out firsthand, and can't believe we've never outfitted our staff correctly."

Grace began an internet search for the required items.

"I need you to change Jason's classification from being a tree chopper to a carpenter and handyman. He is now permanent. Melody is an excellent worker. I want to keep her if you can find a permanent position for her."

Grace was scribbling down the instructions as he said them. "Anything else?" she asked.

"Yes, a pay raise for everyone. Our staff are hard workers. We need to compensate them accordingly. Back paid two months." He studied Grace then. "Is that long enough? I want to do the right thing. Our staff are loyal to the business, and we must do the right thing by them."

"Perhaps three months? And call it a holiday bonus?" Grace said, as she continued making notes. "I guess I'm not going home tonight," she added.

"Do you particularly want to go home tonight?" Nathan asked, his voice quiet.

Without hesitation, Grace replied. "I'm not sure I ever want to go home," she said. "I love it here. The air is clean, and everyone is so friendly. It feels more like home than my own house feels." She glanced down at Penny in her bed, snuggled up next to Arnie. "Penny loves it here too, and she has a new best friend."

Nathan grinned. He couldn't be happier. Grace would stay at least another night, and perhaps he could convince her to stay until Christmas, and even beyond. Not to work, necessarily, but to be with friends. With people who loved and respected her.

The florist shop didn't need her. Mabel had called and reported on Jasper's trial. He'd already proven himself more than capable. Grace had immediately made him a permanent staff member. As she had done from Hardwick Falls, Grace was able to work from Blue Ridge, if that was what she wanted.

Suddenly, Hazel burst into the room. "Supper is ready," she said, bursting with excitement. "Did I hear Grace is staying?" The broad smile on her face told Nathan his mother had been eavesdropping.

"Tonight at least, I think," he said carefully as he glanced at Grace. "You are staying, right?"

He watched as she swallowed back her emotions. "For as long as you'll let me," she said softly.

Nathan couldn't help himself. He lovingly wrapped Grace in his arms and knew it wouldn't be the last time.

From the Author

Thank you so much for reading my book – I hope you enjoyed it.

I would greatly appreciate you leaving a review where you purchased, even if it is only a one-liner. It helps to have my books more visible.

~*~

About the Author

Multi-published, award-winning and bestselling author Cheryl Wright, former secretary, debt collector, account manager, writing coach, and shopping tour hostess, loves reading.

She writes historical romantic suspense and contemporary romance, and cozy mysteries.

She lives in Melbourne, Australia, and is married with two adult children, has six grandchildren, and three great-grandchildren. When she's not writing, Cheryl can be found in her craft room making greeting cards.

Links

Website: *http://www.cheryl-wright.com/*

Facebook Reader Group:

https://www.facebook.com/groups/cherylwrightauthor/

Join My Newsletter:

https://cheryl-wright.com/newsletter/
(and receive a free book)